THE RUNAWAY'S PROMISE

BY JESSICA CASEY

To Mom, For Being There

The sun-faded road stretched ahead, hugging the desolate land around it. There wasn't much to see on the long drive; no wind tumbled down the mountainsides, and there was hardly any evidence of civilization to be found. Jonah fought to keep his eyes open. His brother—sitting in the driver's seat—had demanded they wake up at five o'clock that morning so they could reach their destination by eleven, start exploring by twelve, stay at the mines until it grew too dark for the cameras, and start driving back home the next morning.

The mines near the town of Milhaven were abandoned in 1975. Hearing this made the place irresistible for sibling duo Jonah and Sam —two hobbyist explorers. They drove all the way to this town with a mound of cameras, flashlights, rope, and suitcases spilling over one another in the trunk. It was a full five-and-a-half-hour drive to become the first men to document the interior of the mines since they were mysteriously shut down.

Milhaven was what a mining town became when no city planning or enthusiasm for architecture guided it into modern day. The roads there seemed as though they had been laid down at random, with side roads and streets and structures added as if a child had built the whole area out of LEGO. The style of the buildings differed, but all of them, big or small, were old and had been worn down by the same tireless sun. The two men learned upon arriving that the town of Milhaven had no hotels or motels.

After asking around, they landed in the home of a kind old woman named Mrs. Penton, who ran a sort of informal bed and breakfast. They thanked her, paid in advance for the night and for breakfast in the morning, and stashed their feather-light suitcases down in her basement. It was only a forty-five-minute drive to the mines, which was nothing to a pair of dedicated, self-proclaimed explorers.

After the drive, the two young men stood in the middle of a mining site. In the distance, a network of structures, caverns, and heavy debris pressed into the open side of the mountain. The buildings that had been constructed there so many years ago were rudimentary and broken down, struggling even to bear their own weight. Everything was covered in dust, ash, and scrap metal, all wrapped up in caution tape. The attempt to ward off trespassers didn't discourage the two brothers from imitating the adventurers they'd seen on TV.

"For some reason, I thought it would be bigger," said Jonah, looking only partly disappointed as his head tipped back to get a fuller view of the open land and the mountains that enclosed it.

"This isn't big enough for you?" pressed Sam.

"No, but like, you know what I mean. I kind of thought there'd be ... more around?"

"I'm sure there'll be lots to see inside those cave-lookin' things back there."

Sam gestured to two cave openings in the distance, peering out like two black eyes from the mountainside.

"If you say so."

"Trust me, Jo, I know what I'm doing."

The two young men walked around the vehicle, meeting at the trunk. They unpacked all the equipment they had, even though they didn't know how to work every piece.

"Why are you in such a rush?" asked Jonah, jogging to keep up with Sam, who was already making his way toward the mountains.

"There's a lot to see, and I want to be back in town before dark."

"Before dark?" Jonah looked at his brother with a bewildered expression. "Why though? This place would film so much cooler at night."

"Do you really want to be lugging all this stuff back to town in the middle of the night? Besides, we don't want to bother nice Mrs. Penton."

"You're right," huffed Jonah. "That lady creeps me out."

"What?"

"Well, she's just this random lady who took us in, she's like, always smiling, calling me 'son,' it's like, unsettling."

Sam ignored him. After trudging through dirt and rock, they arrived at the mouths of two caves.

"So—" began Sam, letting no indication of fear slip into his voice. "Left or right?"

"Uh, left. Wait no, right first. Uh ..."

"We're gonna go left first."

"And why do you get to decide?"

"Damn, Jo, somebody's got to."

"Well, then I will! Let's go right."

Sam rolled his eyes. The two men ignored their nerves, switched on their cameras, and stepped into the cave. Even with their heavy boots, walking was made difficult by the slick rocks underfoot. As the day's light disappeared behind them, Jonah's flashlight and the lamp strapped to Sam's helmet became their only sources of light.

"Sam ... Sam, do you smell that?"

The two men turned a corner to find a short tunnel—a dead-end—about the size of a small room. But, it wasn't the darkness or the cold that struck Jonah and Sam. It wasn't even the foul smell. It was what they saw inside.

A white, collapsible table with metal legs stood in the centre of the dead-end tunnel. It was the kind of table that might be found in a school cafeteria or a church basement. It looked eerily foreign in this setting. Strewn across the table were dozens of sheets of paper, covered in scribbles of black ink. A dented, stainless steel coffee mug sat in the centre of the table, and cardboard boxes were stacked around the perimeter of the cave.

"What the hell ..." muttered Jonah.

"What is this place?" asked Sam, to no one in particular except, perhaps, their future audience. He turned around in a slow semicircle so the camera could capture every corner of the cave.

"It's like ... an office? Maybe this used to be where miners had meetings," Jonah said.

"Miners don't have meetings, you dumbass."

Jonah's curiosity surmounted his fear, and he strode past the table, toward the line of cardboard boxes shoved against the cavern's jagged walls. Sam filmed from a distance. As he peered into the boxes, the word 'oh' escaped Jonah's lips, and he lowered himself to his knees.

"Jo? Jo, what is it, are you okay?"

"Sam," said Jonah, turning to face his brother. "It's all money. Like, money, thousands, at least, all small bills."

Sam continued to record Jonah, as shock, fear, excitement, and confusion fought for supremacy inside him. He moved ahead and zoomed in on the boxes of cash.

"How long do you think all this has been here?" asked Sam as he wandered over to the table in the middle of the room.

"Holy—" Jonah stopped himself. Still kneeling over the money, he shifted to look up at his brother. Sam stood stricken, his face as pale and as frozen as a ghost's, with the coffee mug from the table in his hand.

"It's still hot. The coffee, Jonah, it's *still hot*."

"What?" Jonah demanded. "You're joking."

"I'm not. Whoever was here will probably come back soon; we've gotta get out of here, like, right now."

Sam's eyes were steady as he looked down at the boxes. He found they weren't all filled with money. Some of them had guns, some held other mechanical devices that Sam didn't recognize. He sprang up.

"I'm calling the police," said Sam.

"No," Jonah urged in a harsh whisper. "There's no time, we've got to find our way out of here. We need to get to the car now, we gotta go!"

Jonah grabbed a gun from one of the boxes, hoping that he'd remember how to use it, praying that he wouldn't need to. The two men fought to keep their breathing inaudible, attempting to slow their racing hearts. They crept out of the dead-end tunnel, using only their smallest flashlights so as not to alert whoever else might be nearby. Through their heavy breathing, the two men heard footsteps and voices, murmurs coming from the end of the tunnel.

A distant voice echoed off the walls of the cave. "Mr. Evans, really, I could have sworn I heard people moving around out here."

The brothers stopped dead in their tracks, Jonah's arm flying out in front of Sam's chest. Jonah's finger lifted to his lips. They turned around, holding their breath as they watched two people approach from the other end of the tunnel. They were tall, dark figures casting shadows on the men with blinding headlamps. Jonah's eyes met Sam's, and they broke into a blind sprint, the beams from their flashlights strobing up and down the cave walls.

They charged recklessly toward the entrance of the tunnel—their escape. Something unintelligible was screamed behind them, but the two brothers never stopped running. They rounded a corner, getting closer to the exit as the tunnel filled with more sunlight. They were almost out, but the figures behind them were fast, their footsteps loud.

Three shots were fired. Sam and Jonah hit the ground hard as they watched the light at the end of the tunnel grow larger until darkness descended upon them.

1

———

PRESENT DAY

Beverly wandered the halls of her home like a ghost. She walked slower when she passed shelves, searching for things she might have forgotten to pack.

She had eight days left. Eight days until she'd be forced to leave the home she'd lived in for two years. She was purposely distancing herself from the house, slowly cutting ties with it. Beverly had started by collecting all her things from the common areas and stashing them in her bedroom. Then, she began packing away all her belongings. By the time she'd be forced to leave, it would be like she'd never been there at all.

The woman who owned the house—Mara Stone—was a kind lady perfectly befitting her vibrant home. Twenty years ago, she would have never thought that she would end up being a foster parent. She had always been a traveller at heart. She spent her young-adult life completely independent, going wherever the wind took her. Getting older, being unmarried, and not seeing family much had pushed her toward settling down. She couldn't bear an empty house in her later years, so she fostered a fourteen-year-old to keep her company, to keep her young.

On chilly fall days like these, she would sink back into her armchair, a living room full of treasures to keep her company. Cups of hot tea, sandwiches, and prescription pills were always brought to her by Beverly, her now sixteen-year-old foster child. Books on every subject could be found lining the walls in bookshelves, and a dozen board games were tucked away in a wooden trunk to keep Beverly and Mara busy. They would sit together in the living room, watching daylight stream in through the windows in the morning and letting lamplight warm up the living room with orange hues in the evening. Every piece of that house, every book, every lamp, every board game, and knickknack was collected during Mara's youthful adventures. These adventures, as told to Beverly, were remarkable, and, though they were not well documented, they were well remembered.

When Beverly was fifteen, she started to spend less and less time in the living room with her foster mom. That was the year Mara was diagnosed with Lou Gehrig's disease.

The ALS started with Mara feeling weak and short of breath, and the symptoms became progressively worse as time went on. Beverly quickly became the only person in the house able to cook or clean. She didn't mind this; spending time in the kitchen was never a chore for her. She loved to hear the subtle melodies of her foster mother's music wafting in from the living room, allowing herself to experiment with old recipe books and a kitchen full of ingredients.

Today, Mara sat quietly in her armchair with an old scrapbook balanced on her lap, watching Beverly walk in and out of rooms, flip through books she'd already read, and ignore her foster mother's glances. Mara wanted so desperately to say something to her, but she just didn't have the words.

Finally, Beverly moved out of Mara's view, retreating into her room to pack. She had known for weeks that she wouldn't be able to live with Mara for much longer, but for some reason, she hadn't begun packing until today. For almost all the time she'd been a foster kid, she had a bag packed. A grey book bag stuffed with necessities for the unlikely chance she'd be forced to leave on a moment's notice. Beverly called it her getaway bag. In all her time at Mara's house, she hadn't felt the need to keep a getaway bag ready, and that felt good.

She was preparing to fit her whole life into an oversized suitcase and two duffle bags. Beverly had everything stacked in neat piles on the floor in front of her, ready to be packed up and taken away. It wasn't her clothes or toiletries she was most worried about packing, but her art supplies. Beverly's art supplies had never left that house, they had all been bought for her by Mara, and it felt strange to think of those paints, those brushes, those pens in any other context than her home.

Beverly sat on the bed and stared intently at the stack of canvases leaning against the white walls. She needed to take every single one of her paintings with her because any or all of them could be the piece of art that would get her noticed, could even be the piece that would outlive her, that she'd be remembered for. She worried that if she left them in her room, they'd never be seen again.

Beverly was about to delve into her corner of art supplies with plastic bags and bubble wrap until a switch flicked in her mind. It was getting late and Mara hadn't taken her dinner pills yet. She walked out into the kitchen, where she could see Mara sitting in her red armchair. She had a book in her hands, but her mind seemed like it was somewhere else.

Beverly pulled out a tray from the cabinet, set the kettle to boil, and took two small pill bottles down from the cupboard.

"Have you had your six o'clock pills yet?" asked Beverly, staring down at the tray and avoiding Mara's gaze.

"Beverly, could you come have a seat with me for a bit?"

Beverly turned away from her, moving to stand in front of the refrigerator. "What would you like for dinner tonight? We can talk while I cook."

"Bev?" Mara said with a new sense of urgency. Her hands were shaking. She met Beverly's gaze with pleading eyes and offered her a smile. "Just ... sit with me?"

Beverly paused, abandoning the tray on the counter and sitting in the armchair beside Mara. This was the first time she'd looked directly at her foster mother in several hours and allowed her to look back.

Mara had a face that Beverly found herself studying often. She had soft, narrow eyes, a gentle expression, and eyebrows that were high on her face. Mara's long hair fell behind her in tight braids, and framing her face were wispy locks that had been grey for so long they inched toward translucency. Beverly met Mara when she was sixty-one years old and often wondered what it would have been like to know her when she was younger, when she would have been old enough to be her biological mother.

"Can we talk about this?"

"I don't know what else there is to say, Mara. You know I want to stay with you, and you know I'm not sold on this Daniel guy."

"I'm sorry, Beverly. You know I wish I could keep you here forever, but this is what's best for you …" Mara looked into Beverly's eyes. "I just want to make sure you're going to be okay when you leave."

"What does it matter whether or not I'm okay with moving?" Beverly asked, frustrated, but trying to retain her composure. "Mara, you know we don't have a choice."

"I just want you to keep an open mind about him," she said gently.

"It's not just Daniel. Mara, how am I supposed to make a future for myself if I'm living out in the middle of nowhere?"

"You haven't even seen the town, Bev, maybe it'll spark your creative mind," said Mara.

"It's just that … I had this plan. I don't want to move. My life will be ruined."

"Sweetheart," Mara said softly with a shake of her head. "You can't ruin a life you've only just begun living."

Beverly was sure that Mara just didn't understand. She wouldn't ever understand. Beverly's expression softened. "You're right, Mara. I know this hasn't been easy for you either. I know you hate that I have to go as much as I do. You never really told me what's going to happen to you."

"I'll be taken care of, Bev. I'll be fine."

Beverly didn't believe her but smiled anyway. Sometimes people need to see a little faith, even if it's not real.

"But you listen to me," Mara said. "Life is long and the world is a big place, darling, don't you forget it. Please, will you promise me you'll give this town a chance?"

"I promise," said Beverly.

"And Daniel ... he's had a hard time the past couple of years, I don't want you to hold his past against him. He's serious about being a good uncle now, so please be gentle with him."

"Of course."

"And you'll write to me, won't you?" Mara looked at Beverly with glassy eyes, her home feeling even more empty than it already did.

For years, Beverly looked to Mara and saw only the qualities she'd admired—her kind eyes, hearty laugh, wise advice, and warm nature. Now, Beverly looked at Mara and only saw the things she'd miss about her when they would be separated.

"Of course, Mara. All the time."

"You know," said Mara, shifting in her seat. "Your parents would be so proud of you."

Beverly gave Mara a sideways look, but not without the shadow of a smile. "You never knew my parents."

"No," said Mara. "But I know you."

Beverly wrapped her arms around Mara gently, careful not to lean into her frail body too heavily. Mara hated the careful way Beverly touched her, as if she were her nurse. Mara didn't want a nurse, she'd had enough nurses to last a lifetime. Mara wanted a daughter.

When Beverly unravelled herself from the hug, Mara offered her a smile. They both told each other lies that evening, both made promises they couldn't keep. They swore they would be alright—Mara living on her own, and Beverly moving in with a stranger—while they were both falling apart just thinking about it. They gave each other the assurance they thought the other deserved. It was true that neither of them was any more prepared to face their futures without each other, but there are worse ways to say goodbye.

2

EIGHT DAYS LATER

Classic rock flooded in from aging speakers, rattling around inside the truck's cramped interior. Daniel's fingers wrapped around the bottom of the steering wheel, his head bobbing up and down as he sang along. Beverly knew that none of the lyrics he sang were the right ones, but she didn't correct him. She quietly sank into her seat, her fingers drumming against the inside of the passenger door.

Beverly and Daniel had been driving to Milhaven—their new home—for hours on end, and no meaningful conversation had been shared. This was not without effort on Daniel's part. He'd asked her about her old school, her favourite subject, her favourite food, but Beverly limited herself to single-word answers. She didn't trust him and, at the moment, distrust was making him sing all by himself.

Daniel was a young man, with dark brown hair and green eyes. He looked like a younger version of his brother—Beverly's father. Daniel was the youngest sibling, a full eight years younger than Beverly's dad. His rounded face and wide eyes made him look even younger than that. Beverly saw that he had all of her father's traits that she herself hadn't inherited. She had a warm, light-brown complexion, deep brown eyes, and shoulder-length curls. She thought she looked a lot more like her mother than her father and even less like this stranger in the driver's seat.

He reached for the volume knob, turning the music all the way down. Without any music fending off the silence, the truck fell eerily quiet. Beverly turned to Daniel, but he spoke before she could figure out what to say.

"I've gotta fill up the tank," Daniel said. "Let's get some lunch, shall we?"

Daniel looked to Beverly, his face filled with fragile hope.

Beverly nodded in agreement. They pulled into a gas station that shared a parking lot with a small diner. After the old truck squealed to a halt in a parking space, Beverly opened the car door and jumped down, her heavy boots slamming into the mass of mud and leaves caked into the pavement.

Daniel pushed the restaurant's door open, causing an overhanging bell to ring, signalling the owners of incoming guests. The diner was empty except for two people sitting at a table in the corner—an old woman and a younger man—both in aprons, both watching the new customers look around.

The older lady jumped up out of her seat, grabbed two menus off a chair, and smiled at Daniel and Beverly.

"Welcome to Franc 'n' Jenny's diner. Can I get you two a seat?"

"Sure. Thanks," said Daniel.

They were shown to their table, which was on the other side of the room, but still within earshot of the man who also seemed to work at the diner.

"So, what brings you two to our neck of the woods?" The lady smiled. She placed a menu in front of each of them.

"We're on our way to Milhaven," Daniel answered, not skipping a beat.

"Milhaven? Hmm, never heard of it."

The tone of her voice worried Beverly. She herself had never heard of Milhaven before Daniel told her about it, but she assumed someone who lived this close to the town would at least have an idea of where it was.

"You've … never heard of it? Really?" he asked, incredulously. "Smaller town, about an hour south of here, used to be a gold mining district?"

"Uh … oh! Yeah, I think I've heard of Milhaven. Tiny little town. Never been there, never met anyone who has."

Daniel's eyes widened, looking down at the table with a startled face. Beverly noticed this. Did *he* even know where he was taking her? Beverly heard that Daniel was working to get back on his feet, that it was his courage driving him to do it, but this didn't seem like courage to Beverly. Running away to a town nobody's ever heard of was the closest thing a person can do to just disappearing entirely.

"So, for the lady, what can I get you to eat?" The kind-faced woman asked Beverly, probably to alleviate some tension. Beverly ordered the first meal she read off the menu.

"Perfect!" The waitress turned to Daniel. "And for Dad?"

Beverly and Daniel both tensed up. It had been quite a long time since Beverly had heard someone talk about her 'dad.' Ever since her father died, she had the word cut from her vocabulary. People might have said things like, 'my condolences about your father' or 'Philip,' but she never again got to hear about her 'dad.' Even though she went to a big elementary school in the city, all her teachers knew to tiptoe around the subject of her dad, not even mentioning Father's Day. Daniel, a man still in his twenties, had never been called 'dad.' He was never asked if he had kids, much less if he had a teenager.

"Oh! I'm not—" Daniel cut himself off, then exhaled. "I'll have the tomato soup, please."

"Coming right up, sir."

The woman smiled, scratched something into her little notebook, and disappeared through a door. The young man in the corner of the dimly lit diner kept his eyes trained on the two of them.

Beverly felt Daniel's gaze sink into her from across the booth. The lack of casual diner music left a deafening silence in the room, save for the clinking of dishes and footsteps coming from the back room. Daniel looked apologetic, like he wanted to tell Beverly something but he was struggling to find the words.

"Look, I really appreciate what you're trying to do," Beverly said, breaking the silence. "But, I didn't have to be taken away from Mara. I have no idea where you're taking me, but I can guarantee that I'd be perfectly fine with her, and I promise you, there's not a single thing in this little town, which may or may not exist, that I'll be interested in."

Daniel placed both hands on top of the table and fidgeted with the cutlery.

"Look, Beverly, I don't have anything against Mara, but her health isn't getting any better. It was hard on her when she had to admit she couldn't take care of you. So, when she found me and asked me to take you in, how could I have said no?"

Beverly was speechless. Her uncle didn't seem angry, or rude, just … exhausted. Could it have been true? Did Mara ask Daniel to take her? It was easier for Beverly to think that she had been ripped from Mara, rather than willingly given away. Beverly knew as soon as she'd met Daniel that she couldn't trust him, so there was a chance this story was fabricated. But, if his story were true, that he was her last resort, and he couldn't help but take her in, she could at least empathize with him.

"So, you're saying that it was Mara's choice to give me up? She always told me she would adopt me, I thought it was the social workers who wouldn't let her."

Daniel pursed his lips. "Mara really and truly believed that she couldn't take care of you with her health the way it was. And she really thought that I would be able to give you a better life. Especially cause I, uh, you know, got back at it recently, with this new job."

Beverly rejected the thought. She knew Mara wanted her to give Daniel a chance, but she couldn't imagine choosing him over the woman who'd cared for her the last two years. Beverly wanted to rip away every bit of sympathy she was harboring for the young man in front of her, to condemn him a liar, but she couldn't shake the growing sense of pity she felt for him.

"Okay. I suppose I'll come with you then," she said, as if she had just made the decision. Her mind was set. She'd go to this town with Daniel and, inevitably, run away, just like she had from all the foster homes before Mara. When she moved in with Mara, Beverly learned that there was more out there for her than what she'd been offered, and she was determined not to settle for this new life she was going to be given.

After some mediocre soup and pasta served by the smiling old woman, Daniel and Beverly faced another silent hour of driving before they reached the small town of Milhaven.

They were greeted by a rugged sign on the side of the road. The sign was held off the ground with two pieces of aging wood, the words 'Milhaven Population 923' written across the sign. The thick black letters were barely visible on the light-blue background, all faded and worn down by the sun. The only things in the vicinity, other than the forest, the road, and that sign, were the tall mountains on the not-so-distant horizon.

"Home, sweet home," Daniel said.

The thick woods on either end of the street suddenly opened, showing the unimaginably bleak town of Milhaven. The town looked to be stuck about thirty or forty years in the past. There were rows upon rows of old buildings beaten down by the sun, every colour in sight faded and dulled over years and years of neglect. It was obvious that no one had bothered to repaint or remodel. The long asphalt roads stretched out in front of her, laying almost all of the town out before her eyes. Their truck passed a row of buildings, a post office, a corner store, an antiques store—many of them covered in graffiti.

Daniel took a slow right turn onto a street perpendicular to the first to find rows of small houses, all similar in colour and shape. Every house on the block was an A-frame coloured in varying shades of blue, beige, and brown. There was something strange about all of these homes, but Beverly took a while to notice it.

She felt as though she were dreaming for a moment, as if she had noticed some small, obscure detail was wrong with her surroundings, a sign that all of this had been conjured up by her subconscious. Beverly had read somewhere that clocks don't work properly in dreams, and that looking at a clock could alert you to realize that you were, in fact, dreaming. That piece of information rang clear in her mind while she stared at the houses, all almost identical, and realized that none of them had numbers. And, perhaps even stranger, almost none of them housed a car in its driveway. Beverly did her best to brush off her feelings of unease, not questioning Daniel about it—he probably wouldn't have an answer anyway.

After only a couple more streets, Daniel's truck stopped on a street significantly nicer than the others she'd seen. The houses were all two stories tall, all shades of white and off-white, with lots of windows. Assorted greenery—mostly little shrubs and bushes—surrounded the lower perimeter of the houses, a small wooden patio leading to each black door. The architecture was exactly the same for every single house. On this street, there were cars. Parked in every driveway was at least one vehicle.

"This ... is the house you bought?"

"Yeah. Well, technically, it belongs to the company I work for here. It's ours, though."

The house Daniel stopped at was no different from any other house on that block. They were all carbon copies of one another, all touted well-kept lawns and shiny vehicles. All the blinds were drawn, the windows shut, not an ounce of daylight was going into any of the houses. Beverly was confused. Daniel was young, a couple of years out of college, and had almost no work experience. Was the new job he landed somehow so important that the company offered him a house in a nice neighborhood?

"This is it," Daniel said, injecting more weight to the statement than he'd probably intended. He added a smile.

Beverly took a good, hard look at her new home, opened the car door, and slid down to the ground. She pulled her duffle bag into her arms as Daniel took one suitcase out of the back, leaving the other five or six for later. The pair walked up the pathway where the green, pillowy grass lay parted, and they approached the door.

"It's open. The door, it's open," Beverly stated. The black door was left a few inches ajar.

"Oh ... well, it was probably left open for us. They knew we were coming today. Besides, we don't have to worry about unlocked doors anymore, Beverly. I bet in a town like this, where everyone knows each other, the crime rate must be next to nothing."

Daniel pushed the door aside, and let Beverly step through. The house smelled like cleaning products and nothing else.

"Isn't this great? Daniel said. "This house, it's so nice and big … and free."

Daniel looked around the big, clean, empty house and closed his eyes for a moment, inhaling a moment of bliss. Beverly looked around. There was nothing in this house. A living-room-looking area extended out to the left, kitchen to the right. White walls, clean wooden stairs that led to an upper floor, two fresh brown sofas, a lamp—she could count on her fingers how many objects were visible. She was immediately filled with a deep sense of discomfort.

"You haven't even told me exactly who you work for."

"It's for a local family's company, the Evans's. They're a big family here, you'll hear about them soon, I'm sure. They've got me in this great position in their company. I have no idea how they thought I was qualified for this, my friend who recommended me must have really pulled some strings …"

"What will you do for them?" she asked.

"Oh, computer stuff."

"Computer stuff?"

"Yeah," said Daniel. "Computer stuff."

"You get paid enough to get this fancy house for doing computer stuff?" Beverly asked, more than skeptical.

"Computers are important …"

Beverly heard Daniel trail off as she went back to the truck, grabbing one suitcase in each hand, and carrying them inside without saying a word. A small part of her thought that Daniel was lying, at the very least, partially, and she didn't need to hear any more lies. Beverly picked up all her bags and suitcases and scanned the shell of a house. She walked past the empty living space, heaved her things up the steep staircase, and deposited them in the room that Daniel had told her she could take as her own.

A knock came at the front door.

"Holy shit," exclaimed Daniel.

"What's wrong?" Beverly called out, walking to the top of the stairs.

"Beverly! Beverly, come down here!" Daniel called out.

Beverly stepped down the stairs, finding Daniel staring anxiously at the closed door. Who could possibly, already be at the door when they'd only arrived ten minutes ago?

Daniel opened the front door, to find a couple standing on their doorstep. The woman's bright smile was intense, almost alarming. Her complexion was a rich brown shade, and her jet-black hair that was tied in a long, tight braid fell over her shoulder. She stood next to a calm-faced man who carried a huge welcome basket, complete with muffins and synthetic flowers peeking out through the clear plastic wrapping.

"Hello! Welcome to the community," said the smiling woman.

"Oh. Thanks, thank you so much. Um, would you like to come in?" Daniel asked.

"No, thank you. We're on company business, actually."

"We're the Morgados," said the man standing next to her. "I'm Luis, this is Natalia, we also work for the Evans family. We operate the town radio station, actually. We're very glad to have some new neighbours."

Luis gave Daniel a firm handshake that he had trouble reciprocating.

"Well, it's very nice to meet you, too," said Daniel.

Natalia flashed a wide smile and took a deep breath before continuing onto business.

"Now, Daniel, we're here with a message from the Evans family. We were told to pass on an invitation for you to visit the Evans Estate tomorrow. You're to meet them at ten in the morning to discuss your position at the company."

"Wow. Okay, thank you, uh, I'll be sure to be there."

"There's something else," said Natalia. "There was a specific request by the family for a ... Beverly Tailor?"

"Yes, um, that's my niece," he said, motioning to Beverly, who had been hiding behind him.

"Oh, hello Beverly, nice to meet you. We actually have a son around your age, Christopher, but he's not here right now. I'm sure you'll meet him soon. Anyway, we've got to go, but it was nice to meet you. And, Mr. Tailor? I'm sure we don't have to remind you that first impressions are of the utmost importance, so please be careful tomorrow. Other than that, good luck in this town. To the both of you. I'm sure you'll fit right in."

With that, the pair smiled and left, leaving Daniel to call out his goodbye as they cut across the yard to their house. Daniel closed the door after a few seconds, leaving him standing alone with Beverly.

"Was that strange?" asked Daniel, who seemed unsure. "I think that was strange …"

He watched the couple walk back to their house through the window.

"Do you have something nice to wear for tomorrow?" Daniel asked.

"What? I'm not going to that meeting," Beverly stated.

"What?" Daniel spun around to look at her.

"Please, just tell them I'm sick or something."

"No, Beverly. You don't understand how important this is. These are my new bosses, we have to make a good first impression, you have to come."

Beverly thought for a moment.

"Fine."

She couldn't help but wonder if everything in Milhaven was as strange as her new neighbours. She tried her best not to think about it. Besides, Beverly didn't plan on staying in this town for much longer. She could handle a little strangeness for as long as it would take to properly run away.

Daniel exhaled with relief as Beverly walked back upstairs, shutting herself into her new room. It was the first time she got a real look at her new bedroom.

The room wasn't really all that big, but its emptiness, its void of anything interesting or personal made it feel huge. The room was nothing but light grey walls, a bed, a nightstand, a lamp, and two large windows. The greyish curtains were as long and pale as ghosts. The sky peaked in through the curtains, a sea of blue hovering above a small backyard. The only instance of real colour in the room was Beverly and her stack of luggage. Beverly sighed as she looked around the white, grey, and, light blue room. She couldn't bear to live in a place so bland.

Beverly pulled out some clothes, some money, an empty water bottle and an extra toothbrush, stashed them in an old backpack, and pushed it far under the bed.

Rooting through her suitcase, she took handfuls of things and laid them out onto the floor. She looked down at an old recipe book, some jewelry, and a short stack of photographs. Beverly realized that she had never considered these things to be her own, they belonged in Mara's home. They all felt stolen somehow. Beverly winced at how foreign they seemed against the clean hardwood floor.

Beverly took a pile of paper and envelopes out of a small box and laid it out on the bed, making a promise to herself to write Mara a letter tomorrow. Beverly still missed Mara, but her heartache felt different now that she knew she'd been given up of Mara's own free will. She had no idea what she was going to write, but anything would be better than not sending her the letters she promised.

Beverly pulled a dress out from her suitcase and hung it in the closet for the next day. She had made so many promises to so many people: to Mara, Daniel, herself. She didn't feel like she could fulfill any of them.

Beverly resented Daniel for what she thought was akin to stealing her future from her. But still, Mara believed so strongly that he was well-meaning and trying his best. Despite Mara's kind sentiments, Beverly still thought that Daniel's naïveté was reckless. And, what did that say about Mara, who was at home now, thinking that Beverly would be living happily ever after with Daniel in Milhaven? Daniel and Mara, they were both just so hopeful, so altruistic, and so delusional. Beverly began to understand why some kids run away from well-intentioned homes.

3

D aniel called it a house—the place they were meant to go to meet his bosses—but Beverly didn't know if that was the best way to describe it. Looking up at the building before her in awe, she wondered if it should be called a mansion.

Whatever it was, it was tremendous. The Evans Estate was tall and wide, constructed of dark-red brick and embellished with white pillars. A tall staircase made of solid stone dared all those nearby to enter, to knock on the giant black doors and await a response. If somebody was to tilt their head far enough back—which Beverly did —they could see the thick, green ivy that had made itself a part of the estate long ago, weaving itself between pillars and coating its ledges.

Beverly was, for the first time, grateful for Daniel's old black truck. She couldn't imagine having to make her way up the path to the Evans's house on foot. The drive was narrow, unpaved, and surrounded by trees on either side. It certainly wouldn't have been very sturdy underfoot with Beverly's uncomfortable heels.

Beverly hated the way she'd had to dress, with her black-strapped heels, knee-length green dress, and her hair tied back into a tidy ponytail. Daniel had dressed in similar formality. He wore the only suit he owned with a black tie that he spent all morning trying to tie correctly. Both of them felt intimidated by the breathtaking entrance, and even more nervous about what might lay beyond it.

"This is who you work for?" Beverly asked, in amazement.

"Guess so."

"How do they afford this? I thought this town hasn't struck gold for decades."

"They haven't." Daniel paused.

After Beverly and her uncle passed under a stone archway, they ascended a wooden staircase and stood on the doorstep. Beverly looked over to Daniel, waiting for him to do something. He gripped the door knocker with shaking hands and knocked four times. He was surprised at who opened the door. Not a well-dressed butler, or a team of servants. It was a woman.

"You must be the Tailors? I'm Martha Evans. Welcome to town."

The woman who opened the door looked elegant and dignified. Well into her fifties, she looked refined, but no one in their right mind would call her old. She wore a structured blue skirt and a whiter-than-white blouse that made Beverly feel underdressed. Her smile spoke before she did. She had thick, black hair that was tied into a slick, low bun and a necklace of what looked to be rubies that wound around her neck like a thin scar.

"Thanks," said Daniel, who was taken aback by Mrs. Evans. He seemed to know very little about the job he had been offered, and Beverly deduced that Daniel hadn't met either of his employers. Beverly and her uncle stepped inside, following this woman into the house. They passed a grand staircase but had little time to examine it, while they were led quickly into an adjacent room.

Beverly and Daniel found themselves in a grand study. The room was half as wide and nearly as tall as their own house. The ceilings seemed needlessly high for a home, bouncing back ghostly echoes whenever someone spoke too loudly. The room was furnished in whites, browns, and deep greens. Black curtains had been pulled back to make room for a small amount of daylight that filtered in. A mahogany coffee table was surrounded by a circle of dark, heavy furniture.

Artwork adorned the walls, all the sort of empty-faced portraits that made Beverly's skin crawl. The house was quiet, save a hushed conversation coming from another room and the faint ticking of a large wall clock. Beverly glanced around at the cold beauty of the room, and she tried to imagine how living in a place like this would affect a person's life. Then again, Beverly's world wasn't anything like that of these people.

A man, looking about the woman's age or a bit older, appeared from out of nowhere to introduce himself.

"Theodore Evans," the man said with a gravelly voice. He had sparse, dark-brown hair, and eyes that were a shadowy, light grey. "You must be Daniel Tailor. So pleased to meet you."

"Yes. Um, thank you," Daniel sputtered.

"Let's sit down, shall we?" suggested Mrs. Evans, coming up behind her husband and gesturing to a room with a table and chairs.

Beverly was impressed at the maze of rooms in the building, how more and more seemed to pop up out of nowhere.

The four sat down around a square oak table, accommodating one person per side. It felt strange for Beverly, taking up equal space to the three adults around her. The table's surface was smooth, shiny, and high in a way that made Beverly feel shorter than she already was. Mr. Evans's mouth was a straight line, his face nearly expressionless, but what Beverly found the most unsettling was Mrs. Evans's persistent smile.

"I trust that you've found your new home to be quite comfortable?" asked Mrs. Evans politely.

"Thanks. I mean, yes. It's a beautiful house," answered Daniel, trying to choose his words carefully.

"Great," said Mr. Evans. "I'm sure that you will adjust to our way of life here quickly and easily."

Both Daniel and Beverly smiled politely. Beverly heard steady footsteps tapping against hard floors somewhere beyond the confines of the room. She tried to imagine who else might inhabit a home like this, and dismissed the thought quickly, focusing on Mr. Evans's words.

"You see, the way we do things here in Milhaven, we find, can be slightly different to the average business. We'd like to help you navigate these differences, and help you understand your place in this community. We know that we're technically your bosses, but we would like you to consider us as friends first. Understand?"

"Of course. Yes."

"There will be many great opportunities that you should know about for you both to meet the people of our town. Mass is held every Sunday at eleven a.m., and then there's tea and coffee following that. As you know, Miss Tailor will get to spend her days at Milhaven High, a fine school, Daniel, I assure you. You'll have the opportunity to meet her teachers as well, many of them work for us. Town hall meetings are held fairly often."

Mrs. Evans chimed in. "I'm sure you've both noticed in your home that you've got a functioning radio already set up on your counter. You see, this town has its very own radio station, 78.9 FM, and I believe it will prove very useful to you to keep it on while you're not working. You can do that, right?"

"Yes, of course, that won't be a problem at all. Perhaps, um, you could tell me more about the job?"

Mrs. Evans laughed. It was a short and pointed laugh; it cut through the air in a way that made Beverly's spine straighten.

"He's right, honey, you're being terribly indirect. Why don't we talk business?"

Mr. Evans shared a look with his wife and replicated her smile.

"That'll be no problem, Daniel. I understand, a bright young man such as yourself wants to see what he's getting himself into, right? Well, I am very sure you'll be happy with us, we'll take wonderful care of you. You'll get the full tour and on-site training in the coming days, and my entire workforce will give you their best Milhaven welcome."

Beverly had been watching Mr. Evans attentively until she finally gave in and glanced behind her shoulder. The footsteps which Beverly had once been able to ignore were becoming louder and getting closer. Mr. Evans stood up, focusing intensely on Daniel.

"In fact, Daniel, we're able to see one of your workplaces from here. If you'd accompany me over to the window …"

Daniel cautiously stood up, scraping his chair legs over the floor as he did. The sheer number of things to look at in the room lured Daniel's eyes away from Mr. and Mrs. Evans, as his attention flickered between all the different decorations and ornaments around the room.

"Elijah?" called Mrs. Evans, looking past Beverly and at one of the room's many entrances.

Much to Beverly's surprise, a boy rounded the corner of a hallway to meet Mrs. Evans's voice. It felt odd to Beverly, since this was the first person she'd seen in days that was near her age. She ought to have felt more comfortable, but, in fact, the opposite was true. He stood there in the door frame, with dark eyes glancing toward Daniel and Beverly, in a way that suggested that he wasn't expecting company. The boy was dressed up, but not exactly the same as Mr. and Mrs. Evans. He was wearing a neatly ironed, yet untucked blue shirt, buttoned up almost all the way, with lustrous dark shoes, but his messy brown curls looked like they hadn't met a comb in days.

"Elijah, son," Mrs. Evans drawled. "Could you give our new friend here a tour of the estate? She's new to town and is bound to have questions. Thank you, off you go."

The boy offered Beverly a knowing smile and a quiet laugh at his mother's dismissal. Mrs. Evans didn't seem to notice; her attention had already transferred over to her husband and Daniel. The boy didn't seem to care when Beverly didn't reciprocate his amused expression.

Beverly stood, turning and watching as her uncle was led out of the room, Mr. Evans explaining something to him that she couldn't hear. Even though Daniel's presence was hardly any comfort to her, she did feel more uneasy with him gone. Mr. Evans, Mrs. Evans, and Daniel walked further and further away from Beverly until she was left alone with this boy, the person she knew the least in this house full of strangers.

"Beverly Tailor?" he half said, half asked, suddenly many steps closer to her. He had said her name as though he was struggling to recall a memory lost in time. Beverly's heart nearly skipped a beat. She was so preoccupied with eavesdropping on Mr. and Mrs. Evans and Daniel, she only just noticed this boy and his dark, hazel eyes looking back at her.

"You know me?" she asked, stepping backward.

"No. Well, not yet. I was told, though, that we were getting a new family in town, and that hasn't happened in almost two years."

"Two years ..." Beverly's didn't know what to do with her hands. She had always thought herself to be someone who didn't easily get intimidated by other teenagers, even if those teenagers lived in the equivalent of a castle, or if those teenagers had parents who were the small-town equivalent to royalty. There was no real reason to be nervous, the authority figures were already gone. Beverly didn't know why she found her own heart beating so fast when he looked at her.

"Sorry," the boy smiled apologetically. "I didn't mean to weird you out. To be fair, I only really looked into Daniel, your ... uh—"

"Uncle," she finished.

"Right. Uncle. I've mostly been told about him since he's the one who's going to be working for us."

Beverly found it disturbing how this boy, who couldn't have been more than seventeen or eighteen, used the word 'us,' as if her uncle was now working, at least in part, for him. He had this air of total confidence that she didn't often see in teenagers. Beverly wondered how much this boy knew about her, since her story and Daniel's story were now so connected.

"And what exactly is Daniel gonna be doing for your parents?" she asked.

She thought this was the perfect opportunity to try and get some answers because Mr. and Mrs. Evans were far too intimidating to ask, and Daniel seemed to know next to nothing about what he'd got himself into. Beverly grew discouraged when Elijah's face fell.

"You don't know?" Elijah's tone didn't seem to be patronizing or boasting. His tone quieted, and he couldn't wipe a look of concern from his face. Beverly recoiled at the expression, detecting something in his voice that sounded too much like pity.

"To be honest, I don't really know anything about him," she said earnestly, not sure what she was hoping to gain from her honesty. She felt compelled, for some reason, to tell him the whole truth.

"You don't know anything about the man you're living with?"

"Nope."

Elijah regarded her with a curious gravity, narrowing his eyes and watching her intently. Beverly was only acting as though she was entirely unconcerned with her circumstances. In reality, she was very concerned. Everything about this situation came with a level of uncertainty that made Beverly uncomfortable. At every turn, she grasped at anything that could return her to a feigned normality, the way she felt when she was with Mara. The future she had painted in her head seemed so much less clear now.

"So, why are you here, Beverly?" he asked with keen interest.

"Well, I was sort of hoping you could tell me that."

He chuckled. It was a short laugh, but a real one, one that filled the whole room. His hands landed in his pockets, his smile facing the floor as they wandered through the house.

"Y'know, I think it's time I gave you that tour."

Beverly usually allowed her skepticism to lead her decision making, but she elected to follow this boy for the time being. 'She's bound to have questions,' was what Mrs. Evans said about her, and she couldn't have been more correct. Beverly had no shortage of questions about the dreadful new town she was moving into, which now seemed to be as confusing as it was boring … a very undesirable combination. She thought she might as well learn how to survive in this town, at least for a while, even if it was through biased information from the rich son of two old-world socialites. She reminded herself with every step that nothing this boy could say should be trusted.

"A tour sounds great," she said.

Every part of the Evans Estate looked to be refined by decades of use, and yet not a speck of dust seemed to have collected anywhere.

Elijah walked Beverly back through the rooms toward the main entrance, the way she came in.

"So, you're saying that you were sitting there with my parents, who you've never met, and your uncle, who you know nothing about, and then as soon as they start talking business, my mother calls me in to take you on a *house tour*?" Elijah stressed the last two words, emphasizing his joking distaste toward his mother's request.

"That's about it."

Elijah nodded. At this point, he was watching her, allowing Beverly to wander the rooms on her own: flip over books to read their titles, look at artwork, peer through windows.

As she swept aside a curtain, she realized the whole town could be seen from the window. The *entire* town, from its dirt-road entrance opposite to the Evans Estate, to the scattered buildings on the outskirts of the larger communities, was all laid out before her. From this height, it was clear that the town was built from nothing. There were no defining features in or around the town, no landmarks, nothing special. Nine hundred twenty-three townspeople, as the sign claimed, were out there. Nearly a thousand sounds like a fair amount of people before you could see them all laid out in front of you.

"You can see the whole town from your house?" Beverly asked.

She found the metaphor painfully obvious, the fact that the Evans's house lorded over the rest of the town from the top of a hill.

"Yup. That's it. The whole town. You should see the view from the top floor."

Beverly refused to look away from the window, to meet Elijah's eyes. She was unsure whether or not that was an offer to go upstairs with him, and she was slightly nervous that it was. She could feel him watching her, and changed the subject.

"So ... what is there to do in this town?"

"To do? Well, not a whole lot, but you're asking the wrong guy. I spend most of my time up here, on the top of the hill."

"Really?"

"Yeah. But then again, I'm an Evans, so there's always something for us to be doing, always busy."

"Busy with what?" she asked.

"Well, look around. All this is supposed to be mine someday. You know, inheriting the family business and all."

Beverly moved across the room and looked through the next window, taking in the view of the town through another expensive frame.

"That seems pretty lonely."

She drifted off, sensing his eyes on her from behind. She wondered how Mara would react to a place like this. Would small-town life treat her well? Probably not, Beverly thought. Mara deserved so much more.

"What do you mean?" Elijah asked. He didn't sound surprised, or offended, just curious.

"Well, living up here, so far away from everyone else. Isn't it kind of isolating?"

"I suppose it is. My parents don't really think that way, though. We inherited this house from my grandparents, it just seemed to make sense to them that the family who owns the town lives separately. We do a lot of things separately."

"Really?" she asked. "That sounds … restrictive."

He smiled.

"How did you end up here?" Elijah asked, listening intently. Beverly let go of the curtain, turning to meet Elijah's gaze. It wasn't often that somebody was so interested in her life. She found it disarming.

"What do you mean?"

"Well," he said, taking slow steps in the other direction, indicating she should follow him. "If it's too personal, that's fine, but how'd you end up with Daniel?"

"Oh," Beverly said, taken aback. She had felt more comfortable when she was asking the questions.

"You don't have to …"

"No, it's okay. Well, I lived for a few years with my foster mom, but she's dealing with some, um, health problems, and I couldn't stay with her anymore. So, they found the nearest family member that could take me, who happened to be my uncle. He, um, took it pretty hard when my dad passed away ... he basically fell off the face of the earth, for like, two years. People don't know where he's been, I don't even know. He's barely old enough to take care of me, but well, he just happened to have gotten this job in a small town I've never even heard of. It was convenient, I guess, that he was willing to take me in. That was all, really. So, we both ended up here together, I guess."

Elijah was listening intently, and it looked to Beverly as if he were about to apologize.

"And your foster mother, is she okay?"

"Oh, yes. Uh, thanks, she's fine, she's being taken care of."

"Good."

Beverly wiped the blank expression off her face, straightening up and smiling.

"I mean, I'm lucky, aren't I? To have gotten through all that, ending up here."

"You know, you don't have to say that."

For a few hanging moments, nobody said anything at all. Beverly didn't know what to say, and she couldn't break eye contact with Elijah.

"What do you mean?"

"You don't have to pretend you're happy about what happened to you, ending up in this place with Daniel. I wouldn't wish living in this town on my worst enemy."

Beverly, wide eyed, scanned the area behind him, looking to see if either of his parents were close enough to have heard that, wondering if Elijah even cared. They walked slowly down a narrow hallway, with rich wood floors and light fixtures hanging from the ceiling in intervals of a few dozen feet. The low lighting in the hall made the space feel confined, as if the walls were closing in. The hallway stretched out forever. Although there was no way Elijah's parents were within earshot, sound definitely carried in this hallway in a way that made Beverly nervous.

"What are you talking about?"

Elijah turned around to face Beverly, blocking the hallway and forcing her to stop and look at him. His voice dropped to almost a whisper.

"Just spend a week here, you'll know what I'm talking about. Most of the people that live in this place, they've never left, so they don't know anything different. But, you will. I know you don't really have any reason to trust me or even listen to me for that matter, but you should," Elijah moved closer. "This town doesn't deserve you, it never will. Please don't make this place your home."

She could hear his breathing, it was so quiet.

"Elijah!" called his mother, from a few rooms away, breaking the silence between them.

"Looks like the tour's over," smiled Elijah, turning and leading Beverly out of the hallway. They arrived back in the dining room, where Mr. and Mrs. Evans were sitting and talking with Daniel.

Quietly taking a seat, Beverly was forced to sit through more tedious conversation between Elijah's parents and Daniel. She couldn't stop thinking about Elijah's warning to her. She played his words over and over in her head, wondering if anything he'd said was true. She never had the chance to question him, or even to respond; as soon as Mr. Evans began talking business, Elijah gave Beverly a quick smile and disappeared. Beverly immediately felt alone again.

At home that night, Beverly wrote a letter to Mara, just as she had promised. She wrote all about how nice Daniel was, how kind the neighbours were, and how inspired she was to paint every beautiful thing she'd seen in that town.

4

T here was a park bench in Milhaven that somehow managed to be colder than the wintry November grass it sat on; its hard wooden planks were held together with nails and cold metal plates that were lifted about two feet from the ground by short metal legs. The low bench was positioned strangely, so as not to overlook a beautiful park, but to face a wide-open street. Across the street was nothing but a few buildings with no signage. There was absolutely no reason for the bench to be there, but Beverly was grateful for it.

It was Monday, and classes had been canceled for a parent-teacher event. It had been highly recommended to Daniel by the Evans family the day before, during their meeting, as an opportunity for parents to socialize with teachers and each other. Beverly, though, was so shaken by Elijah's words, she hadn't been paying attention. She wished she could go back and ask the boy why he said what he did.

The event was set to begin at one in the afternoon, but Daniel was still at work at 12:56. Beverly was sitting on the stone-cold bench alone, watching no cars pass along an empty street.

Daniel was supposed to be the parent half of the parent-teacher social, but only ten minutes before the meeting was meant to start, Beverly got a text from him saying that something was going on at work. He might not be able to come at all, but he urged her to go without him.

Beverly rocked gently back and forth on the bench, trying to decide whether or not to go to the school alone. She had decided to sit on the park bench until it was time to go, knowing that if she stayed in her home, she'd never go. This event seemed important to Daniel for some reason. She told herself it wasn't Daniel that urged her to go, but the eerie message from their neighbours: 'first impressions are of the utmost importance.'

What Beverly hadn't remembered was that hardly anyone owned a vehicle in the town of Milhaven, so people would often walk in the middle of the streets. The park bench that sat parallel to a street wasn't out of place at all, it was like a bench on the side of a walking trail. So, as the meeting approached, Beverly watched as the usually desolate streets buzzed with children paired up with their parents, making their way toward the school.

As time slowly trudged on, Beverly decided that she couldn't sit on that park bench forever, so she made the decision to go to the school without Daniel. Not knowing exactly how to get there, she followed the families walking in the streets, carefully and indirectly, so as not to look like she was following anyone in particular. For every dozen walkers she saw, Beverly saw one car. There were so few cars in town that people had no problem walking in the street even though there were sidewalks. If a vehicle drove by, people would simply step aside to allow the car to pass and keep going.

Beverly, who had kept her eyes glued to the pavement in front of her, looked up—only slightly—to notice she had reached her destination. Milhaven High School was a wide, one-story building. It seemed to sink into the old, beaten-down pavement it stood on. Its exterior was coated in a deep, industrial grey paint that reminded Beverly of concrete, the cracks in the exterior showing glimpses of the white underneath. There was no graffiti coating the walls of the school; it didn't need it. The building seemed to be destroying itself all on its own.

Beverly looked at the entrance from the other side of the parking lot. A sign had been propped up against the side of the school, with words just big enough for Beverly to see from so far away. 'Gymnasium Entrance' was painted on the sign, in long, downward strokes. All of the families walking toward the building seemed to flock to the sign.

The parking lot was fairly big, even though there were only a handful of cars there. Seven cars in total were scattered around a wide-open paved space, divided into dozens of empty parking spots by wasted yellow paint. Because the lot had next to no cars in it, and there wasn't going to be many more, people gathered and talked among themselves, forming groups neatly within the parking spaces. Beverly walked toward the parking lot, making an effort not to get too close to a group of people. It wasn't easy. She kept her eyes down, trained toward the 'Gymnasium Entrance' sign up ahead.

Beverly didn't see the car coming from behind her.

The blue car came barreling through the parking lot, heading straight for Beverly. She heard the sound of the tires before she turned her head. At the last second, she jumped, scurrying backward, her eyes wide. Beverly threw her hand out in front of her as the car came to a screaming halt.

"Hey!" called out a voice from somewhere behind Beverly. "Watch it!"

Beverly stood, looking over the hood of the car that came inches from killing her moments ago. While it was in her nature, normally, to avoid eye contact, she couldn't take her eyes away from the person who sat behind the wheel. She stumbled backward and took a closer look at the teenage boy who stared back at her with a disinterested expression. His hands were still tightly wrapped around the steering wheel, he had thick, sandy blond hair and darkened eyes. He didn't look apologetic; he just studied her face through the windshield.

Before Beverly had the chance to do or say anything, she felt a hand on her shoulder, turning her away from the car.

"Oh, my god, are you okay?" a high-pitched voice asked from behind Beverly.

Beverly's head spun. She could hardly process what had just

happened, let alone the wide-eyed girl who was standing in front of her.

"Yeah. Yeah, I'm good." It was all she could manage to say.

The girl had golden-blond hair and bright green eyes. Her face had rounded features and long eyelashes, and she gave a sigh of relief at Beverly's assurance. Despite her loud outburst, she didn't want a fight to start, so she quickly led Beverly away from the car that had nearly ran her over only seconds before.

"Are you sure you're good? I mean, you look fine, but about three years ago in town, I saw a man get hit by a cyclist, and he had a *concussion*, and he said he was totally fine, but he passed out a few minutes later."

"No, really, that car barely even touched me."

Beverly twisted her head away from the girl, trying to steal a glance at the boys getting out of the car. Surely a group of boys who would drive so recklessly as to almost hit a girl couldn't be provoked by a stranger's stare, and she could do worse things. Even so, Beverly couldn't wrap her mind around the situation. It was all too surreal. It was like there were no consequences anymore.

"Personally, I don't even like cars in the first place. Big, ugly, dangerous machines in my opinion. I understand that they're needed for the Evans and their employees, that's important, but do you really think that *kids* need to be driving them? Flaunting their parents' fancy cars just because they don't feel like walking. It's so dangerous and unnecessary."

"Yeah," agreed Beverly, baffled.

"I don't know if I've ever seen you before. You must be the daughter of the new family staying in that empty house on Pinebud Avenue?"

That question was even more confusing for Beverly because so much of it was true, and so much of it wasn't. Yes, she was new and moving in, but she had already forgotten what street Daniel's house was on, and she didn't feel like anyone's daughter anymore.

"Yeah, well, it's just me and my uncle staying there."

Beverly thought that correcting this girl and calling herself his 'niece' implied some sort of familial ownership that didn't exist. She was more comfortable with the story suggesting she was the new girl here with her uncle, instead of a new man here with his niece. She was most comfortable with no story at all. No story meant no surprises when she'd inevitably leave town and go back home.

"Oh, cool. Well, I'm Caroline, it's really nice to meet you! I'm sorry your stay here had to start with that near miss. If I were you, I wouldn't pay any attention to those guys."

"It's fine, really. Um, I'm Beverly."

"Beverly? What an interesting name! You're very lucky, I don't think there's anyone in town here named Beverly, so you won't have to share that name with anyone. Like, you wouldn't believe how many Sarahs are here, how many Johns, how many Marys. Me, there's one other Caroline in town. But you're the first and only Beverly! Which is good, because it would be hard to make a nickname out of Beverly. Bev, I guess, if you really had to."

Beverly smiled at Caroline, not really sure whether or not there was a compliment in there. She found it very difficult to follow this talkative girl's long, twisting sentences. Beverly forced air into her lungs, doing her absolute best to make eye contact through the dizziness that still gripped her from her close call in the parking lot.

"So, where's your uncle? Is he coming? I'm sure all the teachers and parents would love to meet him."

"Oh. Um, he's working right now."

"Oh, okay. Those people who work for the Evanses have been working super long hours lately ... but that's to be expected, I guess. My parents couldn't make it either. My little brother has got a cold, and they're home taking care of him. Oh! I'm not sick though, I promise."

Beverly smiled politely.

"We should go in now, I'd say they're going to start it soon," said Caroline. "And you, you've got to sit down! You've probably gotten a fright or something, you could be in shock, I don't want you to pass out or anything."

Caroline walked her to the set of double-doors that lead into the gymnasium. It was a regular gym, if not a little smaller. Dozens of people were standing in small groups, with plastic plates full of finger food and paper cups full of lemonade. People of all ages smiled and chatted: men in blazers having conversations, mother–daughter pairs, fathers and sons picking out snacks from the food table. Nobody was looking at Beverly. Even so, she felt unsteady, which was undoubtedly an after-effect of her scare in the parking lot.

Caroline waved goodbye at Beverly and scurried off to the centre of the room to take her rightful spot in the middle of the conversations, her flowing hair bouncing as she moved. Once she was gone, Beverly didn't know what to do, but she didn't feel like standing alone for much longer.

She decided to stride over to the food table in the back, the place farthest away from the stage. There were bowls of fruit, plates of cookies, tiny little sandwiches, and jugs of lemonade. A lot of work had been put into this spread.

From across the room, Beverly caught sight of Elijah Evans, the boy she'd met at the Evans Estate only the day before. He was dressed similarly to the way he'd been when they met, only this time, he wore a dark-green button-down that was tucked into his pants and finished off with a belt. He stood close to the stage, engaged in a lively conversation with a circle of blazer-wearing adults. Though only a teenager, he seemed to command the respect of all those around him. More than respect, though. They looked to be paying close attention, fully engaged with whatever he was saying.

Of course, Beverly thought, the boy with the rich parents must be the centre of attention. She thought he was a hypocrite. One day he says this town doesn't deserve her, that it's a terrible place to live, the next he's laughing and chatting, drink in hand, having a great time. What game was he playing?

Beverly stopped staring at Elijah. She picked up a plate from the end of one table with a shaky hand, began picking at grapes and sandwiches and mini muffins, keeping her head down, hoping not to encounter anyone too talkative. She figured she could grab a little food, take a lap so people would notice that she at least came to the event, and then leave.

"Hey, it's Beverly, right?"

A voice from across the table dragged Beverly's attention away from the mini muffins and up toward the boy addressing her. She didn't like the feeling of moving her head too fast, it was dizzying and hurt her eyes. There was a brown-eyed boy looking at her, with a long, thin face and sandy hair. It hit her. This was the boy who was driving the car.

"Yeah, um, yeah, it's Beverly. How did you know that?"

He twisted his face into a smile.

"My father works for the Evans family, too," he said, with an unveiled sense of pride. "I'm Luke. It's nice to have another family coming and working with us, even if it's a small family. How long have you been in town?"

"Oh, you know, not too long."

"Oh, then, welcome to town. And hey, just so you know, I'd be pretty careful around that Caroline girl. Yes, she's all smiles and politeness now, but she's got a personality like a viper. You haven't been here long, so you probably don't get the whole social standing you and that uncle have to hold here. You've just got to be a little careful."

"With Caroline?" Beverly looked puzzled.

"Oh, yeah, you'll see it eventually. She's crazy."

Luke's warning came out with a chuckle. Beverly was flustered and had no idea what to say to that. She shifted her focus to the man upon the stage, standing by the podium and waiting as the crowd fell quiet. Beverly and Luke were at the very far end of the gymnasium, and he seemed to be audacious enough to talk through the man's speech. Beverly watched the leader of the school board introduce himself, give thanks to the Evans family for coming, and then rattled off a few lines about the importance of education.

"You know, Beverly," said Luke, taking note of how she turned away from him to watch the speaker. "He can't hear us back here, he probably can't even see us through the crowd. You don't have to listen."

Beverly straightened up.

"I'm not sure what you mean."

"Mr. Williams isn't saying anything important. He never has, and if I'm being honest, I'm not really sure he ever will. You don't have to listen to him."

Beverly furrowed her brow.

"And how do you know that?"

"Well, he's led the school board for nine years, and I've seen him do these things year after year after year. I grew up here. I know just about everything that goes on, I know every person, I know how everything works. I could show you around if you like."

Beverly wasn't interested in Luke's boasting.

"Oh, actually, I've already gotten a tour. Milhaven seems nice."

Mr. Williams kept speaking, as much of the audience's polite quietness began to slip and quiet murmurs filled the room. Beverly looked upward, toward the stage, then she scanned the crowd. At the front of the room, directly below the stage, she spotted Elijah, looking back at her. She could have sworn that they locked eyes for a moment before she quickly looked away.

"Yeah. Yeah, this is a pretty good place to be. Especially you, being catapulted up to the place you landed in this town. We heard about that unfortunate stuff that happened to you before you arrived, being left by your foster mom and all, you're actually really lucky to be here."

"What?" Beverly asked.

"I just said you're lucky to be here."

Beverly caught her breath, disgusted at this boy's nonchalance. He was looking straight at her, confused. There was no sign on his face to signal he understood why her left hand was curling into a fist, why her eyes were steady and dark. Beverly hated everything that led her to losing her parents, losing her foster mother, being taken here. How many people in this room knew that story? Who had told them? How much did people know? She felt as if the boy had just stolen a piece of her and unravelled it in the musty gymnasium.

The room started to spin. Beverly was getting more lightheaded as she caught the sound of her own name from the speaker's mouth. She turned around.

"And a big welcome to Beverly Tailor, the newest member of our school community."

Beverly watched the whole crowd of people turn and look at her. There was no applause, no response at all; they weren't prompted to respond. Everyone just turned and looked at her. A high-pitched ringing sound bubbled up into her ears, her eyes widening in fear. She couldn't help but imagine every single person in that gym feeling sorry for her. They all watched her, standing in their little groups as if they were expecting her to do something. She felt as though she were under a microscope.

The plastic plate fell out of her hand, toppling to the floor along with the uneaten food she'd stacked on it. She ran, desperately pushing past people to reach the exit, and she didn't turn back to see the looks of judgment and confusion on everyone's face. She slammed her hand against the heavy door and burst outside. The sunlight engulfed her all at once, but she kept running. She heard the door slam behind her. As she ran, she found herself nearly colliding with the white car that almost ran her over only minutes ago. One of her hands grazed the edge of the hood.

A memory flooded in Beverly's mind. She had been in the car when her parents died. She could remember the headlights flashing through the windshield, the way her seatbelt constricted as she felt her body lurch forward, the beginning of a scream. Both her parents died that night, and she never knew how or why she'd survived.

Beverly didn't realize that she had slowed to a walk when she heard shouting behind her. The word 'stop' was being shouted at her, over and over again, she heard the word 'no' come from her lips. She raised her gaze up from the pavement, regaining her balance and reminding herself where she was. The footsteps behind her got faster, and Beverly's strides lengthened. The voice called out from behind her again.

"Beverly, are you okay? I saw Luke talking to you, what did he say?"

Beverly recognized the voice as Elijah's, but she had no reason to believe that Elijah Evans would be there, running after her. She didn't turn to look at him.

"Shouldn't you be giving a speech back there or something?" asked Beverly.

"Yeah, I should be, actually," Elijah said, awkwardly half-jogging trying to keep up with her.

"So, why aren't you?"

"Because you're out here. C'mon, Bev, stop walking so damn fast!"

Beverly did stop, feeling the blood drain from her face and the beginnings of tears well up in her eyes. Elijah stopped running as he finally caught up with her, and saw the tears in her eyes.

"Ah ... I'm sorry," Elijah said, and he said it again a few more times, scarcely louder than a whisper. Beverly chuckled a little bit at the absurdity of it all. Mr. Evans's son was apologizing to her because she was crying. Crying for no reason. Elijah mistook this escape of a laugh for the beginning of a sob, and his face fell. Beverly spoke, despite the rawness in her throat—something she'd become very good at.

"Why did you follow me all this way, Elijah? You don't even know me."

"You're right," Elijah said carefully. His words were measured, more than usual. "You're right. I know every single person in this whole town, but I don't know you ... I'd like to, though."

He paused. "If you'd let me, that is."

Beverly looked at him for a moment, her heart threatening to beat through her chest. His eyes were so hopeful, and he wore a fragile kind of smile as if he were hanging on her every word.

"I could allow it."

He smiled, and so did she.

With that, they walked together, silently, for a few moments. Side by side, they strolled away from the parking lot, toward the general direction of Elijah's house on the hill. Beverly didn't really care which way they were headed though, as long as it was away from the school. The few tears that had welled up in Beverly's eyes fell cold down her cheeks in the autumn air. While walking, Beverly took slow, deep breaths until her throat didn't hurt anymore, and she wasn't so nervous about walking beside Elijah.

When she turned to look at him, she found that Elijah seemed foreign there, out of context. Beverly had only ever seen him in his own home. In the context of white and rich-brown coloured rooms, the low lighting did wonders for the hazel hues in his eyes. This morning, Elijah's face was bathed in daylight, the warmth of natural light brightening his darker demeanor. She liked the change.

"People will start looking for you, you know," Beverly reminded Elijah, breaking a comfortable silence.

"Ah, we managed to get a good distance between us and the school. Let 'em look."

"The people here really seem to like you," Beverly said, remembering the small crowd that had encircled Elijah back in the gymnasium. She couldn't help but imagine what a stir he must have created when he ran off to find her. She used her fingers to wipe away tears from her cheeks.

"People don't like me, Beverly. They like my parents. My family pays their families."

Beverly watched Elijah's blank expression.

"Wow," said Beverly. "That's an awfully sad way to look at things."

"That's just what this town is like," he said.

They were walking past the town's only church, the 'church-house' as it was referred to. It was a building painted white that showed no outward sign of which denomination it claimed. The building sat on a patch of soft grass with flower pots placed on the church's humble staircase. It was a pretty building, but in a small, quaint way that didn't really impress Beverly. She thought of a painting she'd done once of a church. It was a great and beautiful building, an Italian cathedral, but the high, stained-glass windows were impossible to get perfectly right, and Beverly ended up trashing the entire painting out of frustration.

"You know, when you gave me that tour, you said something about how I shouldn't stay," Beverly said. She felt uncomfortable bringing it up; it had been such an odd, dreamlike moment. This, out in the crisp autumn air, felt incredibly real. "Why can't I?"

Elijah looked at Beverly closely and pressed his lips together. He turned his head to look behind him, then on both sides of the street, as though he were checking to see if someone were listening.

"When I said that you don't belong in this town, I meant it as a compliment," he said plainly.

"What do you mean?"

"Well, I've already told you how shitty this place is. It's tiny, isolated. My parents have the mayor in their pocket, and the police, too. The people of this town just want money, we're the only ones who have it, and they're willing to do anything to get it. They can't see outside themselves. It's depressing. After half a lifetime in this place, they forget that there's anything else left for them, that there's more for them outside."

"And how, exactly, did you know *yesterday* that I don't belong here?"

"It was just the way you talked about what you've been through as if it's not going to stop you … you've got a real future, Bev, and it's got absolutely nothing to do with this town. You can't stay here forever, you just can't."

Beverly chose to keep walking, looking up from her feet to see how serious Elijah's expression had turned. What could she say to that? She knew he was right, she just couldn't understand how he knew it.

"I guess I don't want that for me either," Beverly replied.

"Soon enough, you know," he continued. "You'll be stuck in this town, just like me."

"I don't think you're stuck."

Elijah's interest piqued.

"What do you mean?"

"Well, I know people don't often leave this town, and that the people here expect a lot of you, but I don't see why you couldn't leave if you really wanted to."

"So, you think I could just run away?" asked Elijah.

She paused.

"Well, hypothetically, yes."

He stopped walking, his smile growing on his face as he turned to face her.

"Then run away with me," he said, not hiding the pride in his voice.

"*What?*"

"Run away with me."

Beverly chuckled. "Sure, right."

"No, I'm being serious," said Elijah. "We could actually do it. We could run away together."

"What, right now?" Beverly asked sarcastically, assuming he wasn't being serious.

"No, of course not," said Elijah, who didn't seem to understand that it was a joke. "You'd have to give me a week or two. I'd need to get all my things in order, I could put aside some money and all the supplies we'd need. I have a car we could take, we'd skip town at night, no one would follow us, no one would know."

Beverly was stunned. He was being serious, he actually was willing to run away and take her with him. She could make it out of this town, make a real future for herself in the city. He wasn't kidding.

"You'd really do that?" asked Beverly, in disbelief. "You'd just leave your whole family, your friends, everyone you've ever known?"

"Oh, right," he said as if something had just occurred to him. "I would do it, but you have your uncle. Of course, you couldn't leave him, I'm really sorry I brought it up."

"Well actually," said Beverly, not having to think about it. "I feel terrible that Daniel has to take care of me. He's so young, he barely knows me, he obviously felt obligated to take me in. He'd be so much better off without me."

Elijah took a slow breath. "It sounds like you're right. It seems like the situation is tough for the both of you."

"Yeah …"

"You still have your foster mother, though, don't you?"

Beverly realized that she hadn't told Elijah anything about Mara's ALS. She had only said that she was doing fine. Beverly had wished that it was true, that she could find Mara and live the rest of her young life with her, like a normal mother and daughter. Even though that might not be possible, Beverly still wanted to see her beloved guardian. She told herself that she would never give up on Mara the way Mara gave up on her.

"Yes," said Beverly. "I have Mara."

"I could take you to her."

Beverly shook her head, incredulous. She couldn't believe the offer. Not that she hadn't run away from homes in the past, but this was different. Normally, in this situation, she'd run away with nothing but a backpack, make her way along bus routes and on foot until she was eventually found, or go back into the system on her own accord. She had never had someone to run away with before.

"You would really do that?"

"Yes," Elijah said. "So … you'll go with me?"

The breeze was picking up now, which added a stinging chill to the air. Beverly watched Elijah look down at her with hope in his eyes. She couldn't believe it was possible, that this near stranger wanted the exact same thing she did.

"Yes," she said. "Yes, I'll do it."

5

The first day of school didn't go any better than the parent-teacher social for Beverly. She didn't have anything to look forward to, except, possibly, running into Elijah at school. She soon learned that Elijah was mostly homeschooled, and didn't often come to regular classes, so there was little chance of seeing him during the day. She worried that everyone would remember her only from her outburst in the gym, because, as everyone had been telling her, first impressions are *so* important.

Beverly told herself that there was no use in putting serious effort into her coursework. Most of her teachers seemed to hardly care at all, and Beverly knew she'd be able to achieve a passing grade without paying too much attention. Anyway, she wouldn't be there long enough to collect her grades. She was leaving Milhaven soon enough, to find Mara. The only thing Beverly had to do now was avoid the aggressive-looking kids.

In math class, Beverly spent ten minutes staring at her desk while listening to her teacher talk about the term 'straight line.' She went on about how every line had to be, by definition, straight, and how saying 'straight line' is a redundancy. Normally, Beverly would find this much passion about something so seemingly insignificant to be endearing, but today, it was just monotonous.

When the students were released for lunch, Beverly decided to walk home, not excited about the idea of facing a cafeteria full of students, and the unlikely prospects of finding an empty seat next to a friendly face. Instead, she ate in an empty kitchen.

After school that afternoon, Beverly caught sight of Caroline in the hallway out of the corner of her eye. Sure enough, Caroline had seen her as well. She came walking, almost running, through the crowded space to get to her.

"Hey!" Caroline smiled.

"Hi," said Beverly, a little surprised at her enthusiastic approach.

"Look, I was thinking about what happened yesterday, and I don't think you got a good impression of what this town is really like."

"Oh, it's okay," Beverly promised, not wanting to explain why she ran off.

"No, actually. I want to show you something, a place in Milhaven actually worth your time. There's a café down toward my end of town called Rosie's, it's the best cup of coffee around, I promise."

With a sympathetic chuckle, Beverly hesitated, but accepted the invitation, pushing her backpack into her locker. There was no need to haul it across town when she had no intention of doing homework that night. With a sigh, she followed Caroline down the hallway and out into the sunny afternoon.

Beverly took note of the excitement that rushed over Caroline. She thought, *This town must really be dull if the simple prospect of coffee with a near stranger could cause such elation.* As she walked, Caroline led Beverly farther away from her own home, toward the opposite end of town, and farther away from the Evans Estate that perpetually loomed over them all. Beverly had never been to this part of town.

Beverly was genuinely impressed with Caroline's ability to talk. The girl could comfortably talk circles around her, chatting about school today, and the weather, and the funny thing her father said the other day. Caroline could speak about whatever was on her mind. Beverly only had to nod, or comment in agreement, or laugh in response. Besides that, Caroline was able to keep up a cheerful conversation all by herself. Beverly found this comforting. She often struggled with small talk.

The leeway in conversation allowed Beverly to look around and take notice of this new area of the town. It was different from the other end of town, but in a subtle way that took her longer to detect. The houses were smaller, built a touch less uniformly, all with different shades of the same few colours. Everything in sight could have used a fresh coat of paint, and the roads were more torn up than the rest of the town. The piles of leaves caked against the curb were mixed with dirt and garbage. This was just a slightly uglier side of an ugly town in Beverly's mind. She turned back occasionally, just to watch the Evans Estate get farther and farther away, almost small enough to disappear into the hill on which it sat.

"Welcome," Caroline announced, "to the home of the best cup of coffee in town. With the best cinnamon rolls, I might add."

She gestured with a proud smile to a small, brown building with glass windows and two black doors that were plastered in newspaper clippings, posters, and other colourful signs. The place had a rustic look, with jazz music pouring out of the half-open doors. The paint chipping off of the wood siding signaled that this café had seen better days.

Beverly pushed in the heavy door and took in the aroma of freshly brewed coffee. For such a beautiful place, she found the outside deceptively underwhelming. Hardly anyone was inside; not that Beverly was paying attention to the people. As soon as she came into the shop, she couldn't help but smile. She looked past the counter, toward the seating area. The royal-blue walls, the soft brown carpeting, the potted plants, the old chairs, and the sofas—it all reminded her so much of Mara's house. This was the closest she'd felt to being in her own home since she'd left.

In Beverly's mind, most of the town had been beaten down by time, but this café carried its history and did it gracefully. Tall bookshelves held hundreds of books, picture frames, and trinkets, the mellow lamplight brought an orange hue to the whole place. She couldn't contain her short burst of joy—and longing for Mara's home

—as she looked around the room. She didn't even notice that the boy behind the counter had noticed her.

"Like it?" Caroline asked, with an awaiting smile.

"Yeah. Yeah, this is a pretty cool spot."

Beverly stood in front of the counter, staring up at the menu on the wall. Caroline walked straight past the counter to a small table in the far corner of the café and dropped her brown messenger bag on the floor next to one of the seats.

"Take a seat, Beverly. Somebody will be over soon."

"Oh, sure."

They both sat down, and their knees almost touched under the narrow table. Caroline went on, explaining every item on the menu from memory, which was the best, which was overrated or underrated. It was very clear, Beverly thought, that Caroline spent a fair amount of her time in this café. She had a lot of pride attached to this place, and she seemed particularly proud that a place this nice was located in the same rough-around-the-edges part of town that she lived in.

Not long after Caroline finished giving Beverly a rundown of the cold drinks and pastries, a boy came out from behind the counter, a friendly face with blond hair, jeans, and a white shirt buttoned all the way up to the collar.

"Hey, Caroline," he said, welcoming them with a sideways grin. His wavy, sand-coloured hair had deceptively warmer, redder undertones in the peculiar lighting of the café.

"Simon, this is my friend, Beverly."

Simon's steady blue eyes turned to Caroline's companion, his expression brightening.

"New girl, Beverly? Nice to meet you, I'm Simon."

In Beverly's experience, being called the 'new girl' was hardly a good thing, but there was no contempt in his voice. Just genuine interest. He held out a hand, which Beverly shook.

"Hey," was all that Beverly said, not aware that people shook hands anymore.

"So, Beverly, I'm guessing you've never been to Rosie's before?"

"You'd be right," she replied.

"In that case, welcome to my own little slice of heaven in Milhaven. It's one of my favourite places, and I must say, you've got a damn good tour guide."

Caroline thanked him with playful modesty. Beverly looked on in awe of the boy in front of her; she had never encountered a person who enjoyed their job and their workplace so much.

"She ... will have a strawberry frappé and a cinnamon bun, Simon," said Caroline, taking careful note of what Beverly had taken interest in while she was listing her own favourites from the menu. "I, of course, will have the usual."

"Of course," mocked Simon, in the same tone Caroline had used. "Um, really nice to meet you ... Beverly," Simon added.

He offered her one last smile before turning and leaving, disappearing behind the counter, and then out of a door leading into the kitchen.

"So..." Caroline said. "You've met Simon."

"Yep."

Caroline beamed with a knowing smile.

"Hey," Caroline continued. "So, I know you're new and all. I was wondering if you wanted to come to a party on Saturday night at my boyfriend's house? At around eight. It might help you to, I don't know, meet a few people, let the town get to know you? If parties aren't your thing, you know, that's cool, too."

"No, I'll be there," Beverly said without thinking, watching that brilliant smile form again on Caroline's face. "Sounds like fun."

Caroline seemed incredibly pleased with herself and continued to tell Beverly all about the party. She went on about how Simon was going to be there, how she's not really the partying sort unless her boyfriend's hosting. Her conversation topics circled until Beverly stopped caring about what she was talking about, and just listened to her pleasant excitement about everything she said. It wasn't Simon who returned partway through their delightfully one-sided conversation to deliver their food and drinks, it was a tall girl with a strong jawline, who was greeted by Caroline with a 'hey, Beth.' This disruption didn't stop her from talking, chatting in between mouthfuls of a blueberry muffin.

After a few minutes of spirited chit-chat over empty cups and crumb-dusted plates, it was Beverly's decision to call it a day. Beverly's eyes flicked over to Simon, who seemed to be mindlessly scrubbing a coffee cup with a towel on the other side of the counter. Caroline agreed that she should get home, and she stacked her used napkins on the plate.

"Hey, Simon, we're taking off now … when does your shift end?"

Simon turned his head over to Beverly, then peered down at the towel in his hand. "Um … how about right now?" he said, stepping around the counter and finding his way to Caroline's side.

"Walk me home?" Caroline asked.

"Of course."

As quickly and as easily as that, Simon literally and figuratively threw in the towel and followed behind Caroline and Beverly. It was surprising for Beverly, to be suddenly surrounded by two enthusiastic strangers, but it felt … nice. They left through the café's narrow doorway, one by one, each person holding the door for the next. The gentle music of the café faded as they walked away, farther away from the school, and farther away from Daniel's house.

"Oh, hey!" cried Caroline at a volume that indicated she didn't care much about whether passersby could hear her or not. Waving her arms, she half-jogged toward a brown-eyed girl with tightly woven braids in her hair, leaving Simon and Beverly steps behind her. "I needed to talk to you about student council. Do you have a minute?"

"Yeah, sure, I've got all day!"

"Hey," Caroline turned back to Simon. "Sorry, I really, really gotta go, could you maybe show Beverly around, or just walk her home? And be nice to her, remember, she's new. Don't scare her away or we won't have a new family for another two years."

"Yes, sir," Simon said, nodding at Caroline's pointing finger.

"I'll see you later, Beverly! Bye-bye!"

Caroline gave Beverly a quick wave and walked off with the other girl.

"Sorry," chuckled Simon, who's gaze had shifted back to Beverly. "She can be a bit much sometimes."

"No," said Beverly. "She's sweet."

"Yeah, she, uh, she is."

Simon was still studying Beverly's face, but Beverly was distracted. She was looking past him, her eyes glued to the other end of the street. She examined a transaction between two teenagers, two older boys in hoodies, one handing something to the other. Elijah Evans's warnings rang over and over in her head, 'this town is dangerous.' She wondered if he was being dramatic. She studied the two boys, trying to read their lips, figure out what they were saying.

"So?" asked Simon, expectantly.

"Sorry?" asked Beverly, her attention snapping back to Simon.

"So, did you still want that tour?" he asked, hopefully.

"Yeah," said Beverly, without thinking. "Um, sure, I should be getting home soon, though."

"No problem. I'll warn you though, there's plenty to see."

Beverly looked up at Simon. She couldn't tell whether or not he was joking when he said that. She detected no sarcasm in his voice, there was only sincerity in his smiling, freckled face. She tried not to give in to his odd enthusiasm too much.

"Okay," he said. "First things first, then. You've seen Rosie's, so, unfortunately, we can't save the best for last, but there's nothing we can do about that. What else have you seen?"

"Oh, um," Beverly thought. She could be honest and say that she had been to school and the Evans Estate. She guessed, though, that telling this boy she'd been to the Evans Estate would be a bad idea. The huge house on a hill seemed so far away now.

"I haven't really seen anything else, to be honest."

"Nothing? Oh, wow. Then, I've got my work cut out for me."

"Alright, let's go."

"So … you've been to Rosie's, the heart and soul of this town. If you keep walking, to your left you'll find the school and the library, but I think we can skip those for now. These are all houses, where people live. We can keep walking down this street, to find more exciting things."

This time Beverly chose to laugh, and it was the right decision, evidently, because Simon returned it with a smile filled with pride. They began walking down a new street.

"So, you haven't seen anything at all. How long have you been in town?"

"Oh, just a day or two."

"And, you haven't seen anything? Hard to believe, but I'll take your word for it. How long are you staying?"

Beverly held her tongue, unsure of the right answer to that question. He must have assumed that she wouldn't be staying long, and would be leaving soon. Funny how that assumption was correct. Nobody else knew she planned to run. No one except for Elijah. Thinking about running away again was exhilarating; she knew she should keep her secret, but telling this stranger the truth was irresistible.

"Don't know," she shrugged. "Not too long, I'm just visiting."

"Okay, cool," nodded Simon, with only a hint of disappointment in his voice. "How'd you end up visiting this place?"

"Oh," Beverly said. She needed to make up a story, so she might as well make it good. "My foster mom and I live in a bigger city, and we were looking for a relaxing place to stay for a week. It's her birthday, and we always take some time off to go see a new place to celebrate."

"Oh, that sounds so nice. I hope you enjoy it."

Beverly hoped she would never see this boy again, hoped she wouldn't have to keep up that poorly constructed lie. Part of what she was saying was true, though. All of the best lies have some grain of truth to them—like how she didn't intend to stay in this town for long, and how she was planning on seeing Mara on her next birthday.

"What's that?" Beverly pointed to a building. It was a shady, white building, its paint peeling off, exposing blackened wood. It was small, much too small to have been a house, but Beverly was a bit too far away to read the sign stuck to the exterior.

"That's the post office."

The post office, Beverly thought, how lucky it was that she asked. Though she only expected to stay in town until Elijah was ready to leave, she wanted to send a letter. Mara had made her promise to write, and she fully intended to keep that promise. She'd tell her that Daniel's great, everybody's doing fine. She couldn't tell Mara that she was planning to run away, that would only worry her. Beverly assured herself that Mara wouldn't be upset with her decision to run away.

"So, what's it like where you live? I mean, our little town must pale in comparison, right?"

"No, it's not like that. I do like this place, it's so ... charming," said Beverly, shocked at the words that were coming out of her mouth. "I just don't think it has what I need, you know, if I were to live here."

His brow furrowed.

"What do you mean?"

"Well, I'm just thinking about the future. I'm a painter, I'd probably have better luck pursuing art in a bigger place, more opportunities, where people really appreciate art."

"You know," Simon said with a growing smile, "I am so glad you said that."

"What do you mean?"

"Well, we've just arrived at our final stop on the tour."

Simon stood in front of a house. One house, standing in line with dozens of others. It was one story, a wide, grey home with thick, dark, blue curtains that blocked all light from coming in. There was no mailbox on the exterior, no flowers growing in its barren front garden, and the lawn was yellowed and overgrown. There was no car in the driveway but, in fairness, there were no cars at all on the whole street. This modest house looked not dissimilar to any other house on the street, except for the fact that it hadn't been taken care of. Not at all.

"Is this your house?" asked Beverly, confused.

"No. God, no, we're not going to my house. This place is a lot better."

Beverly looked at Simon with wide eyes and a furrowed brow, her curiosity turning into confusion. She trusted Simon a little more than at the beginning of this so-called tour, but she couldn't help her body tensing up as this near stranger tried to lead her inside another stranger's house.

"Look, I really appreciate this tour, but I don't think I'm up for meeting anyone right now, like, um, I wouldn't want to impose on someone else's house or anything." Beverly's spluttering excuses rolled off her tongue, as she tried her best to find a good reason why she shouldn't enter this house.

She felt like she was her fourteen-year-old self again, staring down a new foster home, feeling unsafe and unsure.

"What are you talking about? Nobody lives here."

"What?"

"Look, if you want, I can just walk you home, or you could walk yourself home, that's totally your choice. But, um, I really think you'd like to see this place. Y'know, since you won't be in town for too long, this'll probably be your only chance to see it."

Beverly stared up at this house. Even though it was one of the smallest houses on the block, she couldn't help but look up at it as if it were challenging her, its meager appearance daring her to not be afraid of what it might hold inside. Simon watched her looking up at the house's green, wooden door, watched her eyes widen as she bit her lip.

Simon held his breath when Beverly turned to him, ready to tell him how she wanted the evening to begin.

"Sure, let's go in."

6

The house didn't require a key. Simon just twisted the rusted doorknob and it opened. As soon as the paint-chipped door squealed open, distant music sang from somewhere deep inside the house. The music was faint, yet persistent, like a pulse. Beverly struggled to pin down the song title, or the artist, or even the genre. Her head turned to search all around the room, hoping no one was around, that nothing was out of the ordinary. She didn't find anything special. It was surprising to her how unsurprising the place was. It was a modest home, with cold, grey flooring and aging wallpaper. To her right was a living room staged with mismatched furniture, and straight ahead was a small kitchen full of half-empty plastic cups.

Much to her surprise, there were people in the living room. A pair of teenagers sharing a cramped sofa, talking, completely unbothered by Simon and Beverly bursting in on them. They didn't even look up.

"What exactly are we doing here?"

Simon disregarded the people on the sofa and turned to walk down a short flight of stairs. "It's actually down here I wanted to show you."

"Simon, whose house is this?"

"Don't worry," he said gently. "Nobody actually lives here. Well, not anymore. There used to be a man who lived here. He left town all of a sudden a few months ago, and his stuff just kind of stayed here, and obviously there wasn't anyone else to move in."

"Oh," said Beverly, still not understanding why they were there in the first place. "Okay."

Beverly followed Simon down the stairs, toward the growing beat. She didn't know why she'd let a stranger take her down to another stranger's basement, but she was here now and wouldn't turn back. As much as her brain told her to turn back, another part of her compelled her forward. She opened the door at the bottom of the steps to find that the basement was all one room. The place was full of people, mostly teenagers, and was undivided except for a bar, with a smooth countertop and a row of barstools.

The music was clearer now, less distorted, but it was still only background music; an instrumental song, with pointed piano chords dancing atop a mellow bass. It was beautiful, yet muted, like a song that begins to build but gets frozen in time, never quite reaching the crescendo. A gorgeous piece, yet unsatisfying.

The main focus wasn't meant to be the music at all, it was the boy who stood at the front of the room, a microphone stand in front of him. Beverly could tell he was speaking, but she couldn't make out what he was saying with so much distance and so many people between them. There were about twenty people in the room, all teenagers or people not far from their teenage years. They were almost all facing this boy, a teenager in jeans and a green button-up, his dark-brown hair falling over his face as he spoke. His left hand rested on the microphone stand.

People chatted quietly among themselves, their hushed voices blending with the quiet music coming from the speakers. There were girls pouring themselves drinks and boys sitting at barstools with fingers tapping against the countertop. Groups of friends sat comfortably, leaning into each other on couches and sofas that were pushed against the wall. Half of the small crowd was standing, the other half sitting, but everyone was watching the front of the room. Beverly joined the group that was standing, silently grateful that everyone's eyes remained glued to the boy at the microphone. Nobody was watching her. Her smile widened. She didn't notice that Simon was following behind her.

"What is this?" Beverly asked.

"It's just a place to be for kids around here," Simon replied.

Beverly instinctively stepped toward the middle of the room. She found a comfortable spot to lean against the wall that was close enough to hear the speaker.

"What's the deal with the guy at the microphone?" Beverly asked.

"It's open mic, and tonight is poetry night."

Beverly hadn't heard anyone recite poetry in years, not since middle school. She never liked the fact that everyone in her language arts class had to come up and read their own original poetry. There were things she wanted to say, but she could never find the right words, so nothing she wrote felt good enough. Reading her poem in front of the class made her feel oddly vulnerable, even when she felt that what she wrote was never really honest or personal. Drawing and painting felt so much more sincere to her, it came naturally. Beverly admired, from afar, those able to find the right words so easily, especially the boy speaking at the microphone.

"Sometimes,

She falls asleep on my couch,

And I haven't the heart to wake her up.

So I wait until the sunlight spills over her and she blinks awake.

Her bright eyes a thousand lights to lead me home ..."

Beverly watched the crowd's dull roar dissolve into a soft mutter as this boy spoke. Heads turned, conversations stopped. Everyone's day was put on hold just to listen. Beverly subconsciously stepped away from the group of boys huddled by the wall next to her. She came forward, even closer to the boy at the microphone.

"Moments slip away from me,

Like the sun over a horizon,

When I see her, with her eyes closed,

As quiet and still as a promise."

Those must have been the final lines of the poem, because he stopped, letting his silence hang in dead air for a few seconds. In that moment, the one frozen in time, that felt like hours, he met Beverly's gaze. Beverly was already watching him with wide eyes and parted lips. She was taken aback with how obvious his eye contact was, his eyes narrowing, zeroing in on her, his left hand unravelling from the microphone stand.

"Thank you." The boy finished in what was hardly more than a whisper. Instead of ceremoniously walking off the non-existent stage and out of sight, he let go of the mic stand and walked straight forward through the crowd. A wave of approval came from the room, all in the form of snapping and clapping, punctuated with shouted exclamations. Simon looked to Beverly, whose eyes were elsewhere.

"What do you think?" Simon asked, his voice filled with pride.

"Who was that?" Beverly asked, incredulously. Simon looked a little disheartened by the question, but Beverly had only wanted to know how a person as interesting as that could possibly live in a place as boring as Milhaven.

"My friend. His name's Christopher Morgado, people call him Chris usually, he lives a little farther away but he likes this place a lot, and, uh, it looks like he's coming this way now."

Morgado? That name was familiar to her. The poet boy was already striding over, his face just as sincere and welcoming as from the microphone.

"Simon, hey," he said, falling into Simon's arms with a warm but quick embrace, before retreating back and turning toward Beverly. "So, who's your friend?"

"Beverly," she interjected. She didn't want anybody else speaking for her.

"Beverly," Christopher repeated. "So you must be that new girl who just came to town?"

"Yeah, that's me."

"Oh, my deepest condolences," he chuckled, turning around and grabbing two drinks from the counter. He put one in Simon's hand, the other in Beverly's.

"So, Simon's had the privilege of showing you around, I'm guessing?" Christopher asked.

"Yeah, he brought me here."

"Simon, you're showing her one of our town's best-kept secrets on her first day? That's a bold move, man, gotta leave some things for later. Believe me, you're lucky, Beverly."

Simon shrunk against the wall.

"One of the town's secrets?" Beverly asked. "And how many are there?"

Christopher didn't say anything for a second, in the same way that he paused at the end of his poem. "She's getting ahead of herself, Simon. Trust me, Bev, can I call you Bev? Trust me, you'll see more soon, but for now, have a drink, relax, enjoy the poetry."

"I really liked your poem, by the way."

"Thanks." He looked around at a group of people behind him. "Ah, well, I've got to go, but if you need anything at all, my name's Christopher." He offered a sincere smile. "Welcome to town." It was the last thing he said. Simon looked down at the floor. A girl went up to the microphone.

"Thank you, Christopher. Coming up next to the mic, Ryan Lewan."

The room filled with snaps and claps and a rumble of voices.

"So that was Christopher?"

"Yep," said Simon. "That's Caroline's boyfriend."

"So *he's* Caroline's boyfriend?" Beverly asked incredulously.

"Yep."

She remembered where she had heard the name Morgado. Those were her neighbours, the ones that worked for the Evans family, just like Daniel. Beverly turned her head to find an empty microphone stand at the front of the room.

"Hey ..." Beverly said to Simon, who had glued himself to the wall. "I think there's a free couch up at the front, want to go up and listen?"

"Yeah, sure."

Simon's once-faltering enthusiasm fully returned. He took her hand, leading her through the tight crowd all the way up to the front of the room. The couch they stopped at was in good condition, seemingly leather. Beverly couldn't imagine why someone moving away wouldn't bring furniture this expensive with them. She looked around the room, at lamps, a coffee table, a clock, a rug on the floor. This was a fully furnished home, with no one living in it, filled with bored teenagers. When Beverly sat back into the couch, Simon took the suspicious-looking red cup that Christopher gave her from her hands and went to throw it out.

"You'll thank me for that later," he promised after he came back, taking a seat beside her. A boy got up off a barstool and walked to the front of the room.

"Alright, dudes," he said into the microphone. Beverly gave Simon a puzzled look. "I wrote this piece in the shower, hope y'all like it."

This, inexplicably, warranted a round of applause.

"Of the miles of land ahead, your beatnik luminance creates 'affinite' footsteps, of—"

"Is that even a word? I don't think that's a word," Beverly whispered to Simon.

"No talking," he whispered back. "Have you no appreciation for the arts?"

Beverly laughed at Simon, and he smiled back at her.

The boy continued, and Simon tried not to laugh at the very serious poem. But he couldn't help it. His hand clamped over his mouth, forcing the laughter back down his throat, caused Beverly to laugh even more.

"Alright, thanks, that's it, everyone."

The room erupted into applause and snapping. Beverly's back pressed farther into the couch, her fingers absentmindedly tapping against the couch's leathery armrest.

A new person was at the microphone, thanking the last boy for his poetry and inviting someone else to go up next. Simon's attention was drawn away when a girl with long, braided hair and a hooked nose came over and knelt down next to the couch, her hands resting on its arm. Simon shot this girl an annoyed look, and they spoke to each other in whispered tones, so as not to offend the new poet.

Simon turned back around to Beverly, who had been trying not to eavesdrop.

"Hey, I'm really sorry, Bev, but I have to go take care of something. I'll be right back, though, okay?"

"Yeah, uh, no problem. I've got to go to the bathroom anyway."

Beverly needed some excuse to remedy the apologetic look on Simon's face.

"Okay," he said. "I'll see you back here in a little bit."

Beverly nodded, and with that, Simon was off. He disappeared into the crowd of people, and Beverly sat alone. She felt uncomfortable making eye contact with the person standing and reading poetry off a crumpled piece of paper without someone sitting with her. She stood, walking around the sofa and weaving past a crowd of people to try to find the way back upstairs.

Now that she wasn't with Simon, Beverly found more eyes followed her, so she kept her gaze trained forward. She found the exit and closed the door behind her, stifling the music. She decided to leave the basement and go upstairs, not really sure of where to go from there. She didn't actually need to go to the bathroom; she didn't even care where the bathroom was. She just needed to kill a couple of minutes.

The whole main floor seemed to be empty. Beverly wandered around the kitchen, peering into open cabinets and looking through drawers. It was a fully equipped kitchen, with pots, pans, glasses, and even photographs on the wall. Simon had mentioned that the man who lived here had left suddenly, but she couldn't imagine why he'd have to leave a full house behind. Beverly couldn't help but think of Mara's house: a complete home, except without her in it. She could sympathize with this mysterious runaway.

Hoping for a distraction, Beverly left the kitchen and started down the hallway. None of the lights were switched on, so the hall got darker the farther she walked. Of all the doors in the hall, only one was open, and even it was only barely left ajar. She let her curiosity get the better of her and peeked inside.

Opening the door revealed a small room, with eggshell-white wallpaper that had gone slightly yellow with age. It had been a bedroom not long ago, with a dresser and an unmade bed. Beverly decided that this room was a decent place to hide out from people for a few minutes before going back downstairs and searching for Simon.

There was a small stack of books tucked under the bed, sticking out from under a white sheet that was on the floor. Beverly hadn't seen many books since she'd come to this town. There had been the few books she took with her from Mara's, but they certainly wouldn't last her long. She knelt down and flipped through the books. She found a thesaurus, a bible, a computer science textbook, and a few novels.

She sat cross-legged on the bed and balanced the textbook on her lap. It was light and strangely thin for a textbook. Its cover was plain and dark-green with thick, shiny black text. Beverly found that it had been well-used, with dozens of colour-coded Post-it notes peeking out from between its pages, with many sections highlighted and sketches in the margins. At the back of the book were many crumpled pieces of unlined paper, all stuffed between the final page of the index and its back cover. Remembering that the owner of the book was thousands of miles away, Beverly flipped through the papers, imagining they were class notes or homework that had never been handed in.

The first page she saw was a wrinkled sheet, with messy lines of black ink scrawled across it. The writing was long, slanted, structured like a letter, yet it was addressed to no one. Against Beverly's better judgment, she began to read:

There are things I don't want to understand anymore. Like the deals that happen after town curfew, the deaths of the curious. I'm too afraid to keep looking into these things. Far too many times I've been put in danger by my own stupid curiosity. It's time I start ignoring them. I'll never delve into town records again. I won't knock on the doors of victims. I won't threaten to leave

*the town. I'll learn to quiet myself. I will give my condolences to the
parents of—*

"Beverly?" A voice called out, coming from the kitchen.

Beverly's head whipped around, her hands still clutching the book, eyes wide. She shut the book, not allowing herself the time to take out the letters. She tossed the book under the bed and stood up, creeping out of the room and hoping that nobody had seen her. She was both focusing on the voice that had just called out to her and beginning to process what she'd read. Quietly closing the door behind her, she walked back toward the kitchen, her heart pounding.

Beverly found Simon in the living room.

"Hey! Uh, sorry about that, it was just a thing about a school project, um, want to come back downstairs with me?"

Beverly couldn't stop thinking about the note she'd just read: ... 'deaths of the curious.' She wished she had kept the letters, stuffed them in her pocket and ran home, but they were still there. She could probably go back and get them if she thought of a good enough excuse, but Simon stood there looking at her, waiting.

"I, um, I actually think I need to be getting home now. Daniel, my uncle, he won't know where I am. Thanks, though, really, thanks so much for showing me this place. I, uh, I'll see you around I guess."

Beverly managed a quick flash of a fake smile and turned to walk toward the door. Her trembling hand clutched at the cool metal of the doorknob.

"I'll see you—" Simon blurted out quickly, just before the door slammed shut.

Beverly ran home, not caring how she looked doing it. She just had to run. She didn't exactly know her way back home, so her thoughtless running was of very little use. She barreled down the streets, not caring about what any passersby might think of her.

As soon as she cleared the front door of the house, she ran to her room, as if she were running from something, but didn't know what. Her hands covered her face as she sat, sinking into the bed.

That letter sparked more questions than it answered. Who was this man who left town so quickly? What did he mean by 'the deaths of the curious'? What did the rest of the note say? Beverly considered going back to the house on that unnamed street to retrieve the letter, to search for more like it, but that would require going back through the streets of the town, which didn't even feel like an option. This town must be just as dangerous as Elijah had told her it was, just as corrupt. She prayed that Elijah would be ready to skip town soon.

But, if this were all true and this town was really dangerous and corrupt, how could she have just had such a nice afternoon? Caroline had been so sweet to her, Simon was so kind. There were clearly people in this town capable of putting others before themselves. They had poetry readings and friendships and fascinating lives, in a town Elijah thought was dull and insufferable. Beverly felt as though all the information she had was contradictory; she couldn't tell what was the truth and what wasn't.

Someone knocked three times against the glass of her window, and Beverly's eyes flew open. Her whole body lurched forward in fear. Frantically, she turned to the window.

Two hands grabbed the bottom of the window and pulled upwards. Much to her surprise, Elijah Evans climbed through the window, peering in at her with an apprehensive smile. She stumbled backward, her mouth agape.

"Oh! Sorry, sorry, I didn't mean to scare you," Elijah said.

"Holy shit, what are you doing?"

Elijah used the windowsill for balance, landing softly on his feet against the wooden floor.

"I needed to ask you something …" Elijah started, before immediately becoming distracted, looking all around the room as a gentle smile crept on to his face. Incredulously, Beverly walked around Elijah, poking her head out of the window and then turning back to him. With her surprise wearing off, the knowledge that Elijah was right there looking at her set in. She chuckled.

"How did you get up there, how'd you know where I live?"

"Remember, my parents technically own this house. And there's a ladder outside. Look, I really didn't mean to scare you—"

"It ..." Beverly began. "No, it's okay. What's so important you need to tell me?"

"Well, I need a favour." Elijah wandered over to the desk in the corner of the room and sat back in a chair.

"So ..." he continued. "My parents are having a big party this weekend, and I can bring a guest. It's kind of a formal affair. You're coming with me. It won't be too long. You'll make an appearance, I'll introduce you to a few people, then you can go home."

The last place Beverly ever wanted to go again was the Evans Estate. Her first time there was paralyzingly awkward. She was at odds with every single aspect of that place. She found herself uneasy under its high ceilings and among its ornate walls, as well as being in the chilling presence of Mr. And Mrs. Evans. She imagined being in a room filled with Mr. and Mrs. Evanses, all socializing and clinking glasses of champagne; the thought of it made her skin crawl. Elijah Evans was standing in front of her, expecting a response. She wondered what exactly he could gain by choosing her as his guest, but he looked adamant enough about having her there.

"I'm just not sure ..." Beverly said.

"Not sure about what?"

"Would your parents even want me there?"

"They might not, but that doesn't matter. I want you there. Besides, it's not like my parents have any reason to dislike you."

"Doesn't feel that way."

"Come on, Bev, these galas my parents have are all clients and potential investors, they're tedious. I'm honestly not sure if I can make it through without you. And, this close to freedom would be a terrible time to die of boredom."

Beverly smiled at the way his face lit up when he said 'freedom,' even through his veil of sarcasm. If this was the cost of running away with Elijah—just a quick favour and she'd be out of town, back with Mara—it would be worth it.

"Okay. Okay, fine, I'll go."

Elijah looked as though he were about to thank her, but instead, began glancing all around the room. Beverly's room had changed a lot since she first moved into the place. Her suitcase had been unpacked and deposited into the basement. Her clothes were stacked in the closet, her belongings sprinkled around the room. The once-empty space between four walls seemed to be surrendering to Beverly's personality and showing the signs of comfort one might normally find in a bedroom. Photographs, pens lying around, books stacked in a shelf, a half-filled cup of water at her bedside.

The biggest change that Beverly made to the room was her artwork. Pages and pages of old sketches were stacked on the floor with pencils of all sorts on top of them. Canvases lacquered with bright, colourful landscapes leaned against the walls. Elijah's eyes flicked over the paintings, looking briefly at each one.

"Why didn't you tell me you were an artist?"

Beverly raised her eyebrows involuntarily, taken aback by his question. The fact that she was an artist was always something that the people in her life just knew. It was as much a part of her identity as her age or her eye colour. The only people she spent much time with knew and accepted her passion, so she rarely had to justify her art to other people. She supposed she should be excited to show new people her artwork. The hint of amusement in Elijah's voice perplexed Beverly, so she didn't know exactly what to say next.

"I guess you didn't ask."

"Oh, Beverly … you can't spend your whole life waiting for people to ask you the right questions."

His slow words hung in the air as Beverly sat and shoved backward onto her bed, thrown off by his sudden solemnity. Before she could answer, Elijah was already on his feet, wandering around her room, examining each painting up close. He seemed critical of each notebook sitting on the edge of her dresser, each pair of socks lying on the floor. Beverly didn't feel the need to respond to his comment since he seemed to have already moved past it.

"Sorry about the mess …" Beverly mentioned. She often automatically apologized for the state of her room, even if it wasn't that bad. Mara never minded it, though. She loved seeing Beverly's room littered with papers and pens and artwork and books. She said it was a sign of life inside the house. Beverly thought of her bedroom at Mara's home, now empty.

"No, it's …" Elijah struggled to find his words, something Beverly had never seen him do before. "It's not that."

He moved across the room and sat next to her.

"I want to make sure that you don't get too … connected to this place. We're going to make it out of here soon, remember? If you start laying down roots, it's going to be a lot harder to leave."

Beverly suddenly understood what Elijah was looking at. Not her artwork, but the fact that it had been unpacked. This didn't look like the bedroom of someone who was planning on running away. This looked like a normal teenager's room.

"Sorry, I didn't mean to do that. You're right though—"

"No, it's okay, don't apologize to me. It just isn't safe for you to stay here for too long, and I want to make sure that when we leave, you don't have any regrets."

"Well, I just thought that packing up already would look a little suspicious." Beverly made the excuse up on the spot.

He smiled. "You're right … didn't mean to make a big deal of it. So, I'll see you Saturday night, then?"

"Yeah. Yeah, I'll be there."

"Good, wear something nice. I'll see you then."

Elijah stood up and stepped around the bed, exiting through the door. Beverly sat watching the floor, as she listened to his footsteps descend the staircase. She let out a breath when he opened and then closed the front door, and relaxed. That night, she found it hard to sleep in a bed that didn't feel like hers anymore.

everly dreamed about Mara that night. It was nothing special, no outlandish dream that she'd have to spend her first hour awake analyzing. The dream was simple—just her and Mara at home again. Beverly didn't think this was the kind of dream she'd have to wonder about. There was no need to figure out some cryptic meaning, because she was meant to be with Mara again. And soon enough, she'd be back with her.

As soon as the pleasant memory of her dream dissipated from her mind, something else overcame Beverly's thoughts: what she had found yesterday, the message in the textbook. Its words had shaken her, and what scared her most was the fact that there was more of them. There was an entire stack of those papers still lying under the bed in that odd, abandoned house. Everything was telling her to forget about it, and Elijah had told her not to complicate things before they left, but she couldn't help herself. She was either too curious or too afraid to drop it.

Thinking back to the poetry reading yesterday, she remembered that the strange, abandoned house wasn't even locked. She let out a small gasp.

Beverly crawled out of bed and began to get ready for school, getting dressed and stuffing her books back into her backpack. She ran down the stairs, picked an apple up from a bowl, and turned to leave for school.

"Stop!" exclaimed Daniel, from the kitchen. "Don't leave yet, I've got waffles on. The first batch'll be ready in five or ten minutes."

Beverly glanced over to the kitchen, which was full of bowls and utensils, all covered with batter. Daniel was wearing an apron and had a hopeful smile on his face.

"I'm gonna be late for school, Daniel," said Beverly.

His smile faded, and he looked confused. "What do you mean? School doesn't even start until 8:45, you've got plenty of time."

"School starts at 8:30, actually."

"Oh," said Daniel, looking at his waffle maker, defeated.

"Why don't you put them in the fridge when they're done? I'll have them when I get home today."

"Oh. Oh, okay, sure."

It was a lie. School did start at 8:45, but Beverly didn't plan on going to school that morning.

Beverly convinced herself that she had to go back to the abandoned house, and if it was unlocked, she'd take the book. She planned to do it during school hours, because it was so close to the school, and because that was her best bet for finding the place empty. That was, of course, assuming that nobody skipped school today to hang out there. She prayed she would be the only rebel in town today.

The entire walk to the abandoned house was spent trying to avoid eye contact with anyone who happened to be on the streets. She remembered Simon's tour, the lies she had told him, that she was here on a short vacation with her foster mother. How long would it take before he found out that wasn't true? Hopefully, if Elijah was ready to leave soon enough, that lie wouldn't matter.

Finally, she arrived at the abandoned house at the end of the street, just past the school. Trying to look as inconspicuous as possible, she walked up its steps and turned the doorknob. When it opened, she let out a sigh of relief.

She stepped inside, quickly and quietly shutting the door behind her. The house was silent, and it didn't seem like there was anyone inside. Being there felt different when there wasn't music coming up from the basement. It felt emptier and its silence was unsettling. She didn't feel as though she was at a party, or a poetry reading, or a teen hangout. She felt as though she were breaking and entering into someone's home.

Taking a right at the kitchen, she dashed down the hallway and found the room she had ducked into the day before. It felt more like an intrusion now than yesterday, since she knew that she was setting out to read a grown man's private writing, but she imagined that, wherever the man was now, he wouldn't mind.

To justify her curiosity, Beverly thought of these papers not as diary entries, but as clues. Suddenly, she was a detective in a novel or a movie, and she was cracking a code to solve the crime, whatever crime may or may not have occurred in this town. It was her duty to find out, or at least to try.

She spread all of the sheets out on the floor, deciding that it would be best to put them in order rather than reading them at random. She started with the earliest entry, July 25th, and laid them all out, all the way to August 19th, the last entry.

There were about fourteen entries, all about half a page. He wasn't a daily writer, but fairly regular nonetheless. Beverly kept a journal at one point, but she gave it up after only two weeks. She found recounting the events of her own life incredibly boring.

She closed the door behind her, but did nothing else to ensure she wouldn't get caught snooping. She simply hoped nobody would come in. Clearing her mind, she went to work. Beverly started by reading the first entry, skimming it for relevant information, but bracing herself for the worst:

It's my first day in the town of Milhaven. It's rather small and looks to be a little dull, but I have high enough hopes for it. I suppose that small doesn't mean bad. I kind of like how time moves at such a relaxed pace, how nobody knows me. There's a new life for me here.

Beverly stopped reading for a moment. It was such a normal diary entry. It didn't seem like something she needed to skip school or risk getting in trouble to read. She remembered the words from the entry yesterday, about the 'deaths of the curious.' She wanted to skip ahead, but she resisted the urge. She was going to do this right.

She kept reading through the first entry, how it went on and on about how he was happy to be in Milhaven: a new life, being very excited, and so on. The ending of the entry read, simply: 'Work begins tomorrow morning. Early to bed tonight.' He signed it 'Stephen' at the bottom.

Simon hadn't mentioned his name. Putting aside that sheet, Beverly moved on to the next. She found they got shorter as they went on:

Got to meet my bosses today. Their house is ridiculously nice, it was basically a mansion. I have no idea how much money their business makes, but it's gotta be a lot. They haven't told me much, yet, about that sort of thing. I only really got a tour, and all I know is that I'll be handling the computer stuff.

Beverly stifled a gasp, even though she was alone. This man, Stephen, worked for the Evans family as well. She read on, more fascinated with this than with any book she'd ever read:

They knew about my history with drugs, how that's in my past and all, but I was so surprised that they didn't ask more about it. Like, I was glad they didn't hold it against me, but still, I thought they'd at least mention it. I feel like most employers would ask. They almost seemed more interested in me on the phone, hearing that I recovered from substance abuse.

Beverly's eyebrows raised, and she began reading faster and faster, learning more about this man on the other side of the pen. He seemed strikingly similar to Daniel. He was a twenty-seven-year-old man with a computer science background, and he was in Milhaven because it was the only job he could find. Judging by his writing and his house, Beverly guessed that he was single and lived alone.

Besides his past, everything in the entries was fairly tame, fairly normal, until August 9th. That's when the writing changed:

I'm beginning to think there's something a little off about the company I work for. There seems to be some under-the-table exchanges of money going on, and I don't know a lot about big business or anything, but it doesn't seem legal. I'm just an IT guy, and probably wouldn't get into any real trouble if somebody got caught, but still. Something just feels wrong.

She looked to the next entry, which was dated a few days later:

I was right. It's definitely not legal. I don't know how they're doing it, or exactly what they're doing, but drugs are leaving this town in those shipments. They don't seem to have come from any outside source. The drugs must have been made here somewhere. How did I not notice they were cooking here? If they get caught, I'm definitely gonna be an accomplice to drug trafficking. I can't just quit, though. I could probably be arrested just for working here, but I can't get out without them using it against me. I can't have them blackmail me. I'll just have to keep working here until I can find a reasonable excuse to move away, something believable. I'll figure it out.

Beverly's hand was clasped firmly over her mouth. She didn't know whether or not she could believe this writing, but there was no reason for someone to lie in their own diary. It all made so much sense to her. That must be the reason nobody leaves town. They've all, in some way or another, been involved in the illegal activity—drugs, it seemed like—or at least complicit in it. The Evans family was criminal, and the entire town was populated with accessories to their crimes. She read on, skipping to the next entry, dated a few days after the last:

There's almost nothing I can prove, but I think O'Reilly's death wasn't an accident at all. I think they killed him. I'm the tech guy, so I'm invisible. I get to see a lot. I've seen what he's doing on his computer. He was an accountant, but he was moving money around on the inside. A few days ago, his house burned down, and I don't think it was an accident. There are these people, the higher-up guys, who are close to Mr. Evans. They tend to lurk around accounting and the other branches a lot. I asked my boss what their jobs are, what they're meant to do, and all he said was that they protect the company. I think it was them, they must have burned his house down when he was asleep, I don't believe he left the oven on. Again, I don't know if I should be writing this, if it will incriminate or exonerate me, but if I make a wrong step, and they burn my house down too, these pages will go up with it.

Beverly's grip on the page tightened as she looked down at the words. The writing got more slanted as the letter went on, messier, as though he had been writing faster and faster.

Could it have been true? Elijah told her that living in this town was dangerous, but this was completely different. This was murder, at least, alleged. Or did Elijah even know about any of this, the severity of the danger? He was only a teenager. His parents could be leaving him in the dark. She thought that because Elijah had opened up with her so much, offered her an escape, given her a warning, he'd probably told her everything he knew. *So*, she thought, *he must not know*. She moved on to the next entry, dated a few days later. It was the one she had looked at the day before, the one that scared her:

There are things I don't want to understand anymore. Like the deals that happen after town curfew, the deaths of the curious. I'm too afraid to keep looking into these things. Far too many times I've been put in danger by my own stupid curiosity. It's time I start ignoring these thoughts. I'll never delve into town records again. I won't knock on the doors of victims. I won't threaten to leave the town. I will learn to quiet myself. I'll give my condolences to the parents of the victims, and I'll make sure that the inner circle doesn't suspect me any more than they probably already do. I should never have gone to that mine. I've got to stop getting involved, because it's the only way I'll get out of this town alive.

There was only one excerpt left, from the very next day:

I think I know how to escape this town. Yes, they have blackmail information on me, but I know about their enterprise, I have stuff on them as well. What I need to do is get some undeniable evidence of them breaking the law, something I can use as leverage. Something that, if they try and go after my family, or try and blackmail me into coming back, I'll use to threaten to expose them to the police. I think I know how to do it. Tomorrow.

That was the last piece of writing. The house was still standing, and not in ashes, meaning he must have succeeded in getting his leverage. What evidence did he find?

Beverly didn't know if she needed to be afraid, as serious as the situation was. Mentally, she was already in Elijah's car, driving to Mara's house, free as a bird. But, the reality of the situation was beginning to seep into her mind. She might not have anything to do with this town's company, but Daniel did. She had her one-way ticket out of Milhaven, but he didn't. She didn't know if she could escape in a car and leave Daniel alone, because his fate could be much worse than Stephen's.

She put all of the pages back into a stack, placed them back in the textbook, and closed it. She wanted to bring them back home with her but decided that it was way too risky. Instead, she put the book where it was unlikely to be found. She stepped around to the other side of the bed, lifted up the mattress, and tucked it in between the mattress and the bed frame. She promised herself she wouldn't return to that house unless it was entirely necessary.

She left the house just as third period was about to begin and walked to school. She wanted to make at least a few of her classes today, but her mind was straying away from coursework.

After school, Beverly went straight home. She threw her book bag down on the couch and found Daniel sitting at the kitchen table. He was sipping from a can of soda and staring absent-mindedly out the window.

"Hey, Beverly, how was school?" he asked good-naturedly.

"Um, great. How was work?"

He thought about that for a moment.

"Great."

Beverly smiled and sat down next to him at the table. It was the first time since the drive to the Evans Estate that they were sitting next to one another. At meals, they usually ate separately in front of the television or at different times from each other entirely.

"Daniel, how much do you know about your bosses?" She knew she was testing dangerous waters and decided to be strategic in her wording.

"Well, y'know, they're my bosses, we're not supposed to be best friends. I know them, like, enough."

"But, don't you think that there's something a little off about this town?"

His eyes narrowed. "I don't really know what you're talking about."

"Look, um …" She was trying to decide whether or not she should just be honest with him. "I found something, there are these old diary entries, they look legit and they say some pretty scary stuff about the Evans family."

"Diary entries? Where'd you find them?"

He looked confused and leaned forward in his chair slightly.

"Well, there's this old, abandoned house at the end of the street, it's where—"

"Somebody's *house*?"

"Nobody *lives* there or anything."

"I don't care! You can't go breaking and entering into houses Beverly, we've been in this town for four goddamn days! You wanna get arrested?"

"But, what I've found, Daniel, it's really serious, I think the Evans family is full of criminals, they're definitely hiding stuff, I can't prove it, but—"

"But, you can't. Beverly, the Evans family took me in when nobody else would. Nobody. They're my last chance, a chance to make a life here. We can't throw it away on a hunch."

"But, it's serious, I think there's real danger here, I think people've been killed here."

"Killed? No, Bev, nobody's been killed. The Evans may have enemies, but they don't kill people."

"You know?" Beverly accused.

Daniel paused. "What are you talking about?"

She gave her uncle a hard look, and Daniel glanced around the room.

"Look," Daniel said. "I mighta had some suspicions. But I really just do the computers, so whatever minor under-the-table work they're doing, I really have nothing to do with it. Besides, they're not the mafia, for God's sake, it's not like they're doing anything that bad, it's fine."

"If you thought it might be illegal, why did you come here?" Beverly asked.

He looked down at his hands.

"Bev, I need this job. And this house. Nobody knows me here, this is my one shot. There's no other way I can make ends meet to take care of you."

Beverly shook her head. "Why did you feel this need to take me in, anyway?"

Daniel thought for a moment.. "Y'know, your father was quite a bit older than me. When I was your age, and our parents were going through their divorce, he was the one that stayed with me. And, when my dad passed and Mom was drinking, he took care of me. So, when your father passed away, I just wanted to be there for you."

Beverly nodded, wishing desperately that she knew what to say.

Daniel's eyes were glassy. "Besides," he said, gathering himself, "I needed some responsibility, I think, to get myself back on track. Having people count on me, I haven't had that in a couple years. I think, uh, I think it's good for me."

"That's good," she said, not sure what exactly to say. "I, um, I know this can't be easy for you, I appreciate what you're doing. Sorry if I was rude earlier."

He smiled.

She continued. "But, if you knew for a fact that this town was too dangerous to live and work in, we'd leave, right?"

"Uh, yeah, well, of course."

It became clear to Beverly that she had a job: to prove to Daniel that he needed to leave town. No, not a job—an obligation. She already had an escape from Milhaven; she would be home in a week or two. But what about him? As she walked upstairs, everything became crystal clear to her. She would have to free her uncle, the same way Stephen got free, because Daniel definitely couldn't do it for himself.

Beverly knew that leverage was necessary to escape town, but Stephen's letters didn't leave her with any clue as to *how* he did it. She would have to find evidence, somehow, more than Stephen's letters, proving that the Evans family needed to be locked up before they could hurt anybody else. Beverly had run into Elijah's offer of escape out of pure dumb luck, and she thought that Daniel deserved a chance, too.

8

B efore they died, Beverly's parents were beginning to worry that she was too shy and needed to be more outgoing. Naturally, they put her in acting classes. She was stuck in the basement of a church with an eccentric lady and about twenty other children whose parents had the same hopes as the Tailor family. At the end of the year, they had a performance. It brought nothing but joy to her adoring parents in the audience, but it brought nothing but stress to Beverly.

During one performance, Beverly had been assigned a quick change. She had about forty-five seconds to change out of oversized hospital scrubs and into a plain black dress and get back onstage. She had never been so stressed in her life. She worried that she'd forget her lines in the next scene, that she'd misplace pieces of her costume, that she wouldn't be able to change in time. Eight-year-old Beverly stood over the prop table for hours, staring at it, meticulously organizing and reorganizing her costumes, writing a list of stage directions to remember, practicing the quick change at home. She had everything prepared perfectly, and still, she was nervous.

Tonight sort of reminded her of that performance. She had promised Elijah that she'd go to his parents' gala on the same night of Christopher's party. She was determined to make it to both of them.

She had to fulfill her promise to Elijah so she could stay in his good books, but she also wanted to go to Christopher's party. She figured she could try and find evidence of the town's wrongdoings that night, and she'd improve her chances of finding something valuable if she attended both parties.

Complicating things, Daniel had received an invitation to the gala as well, and certainly wouldn't approve of Beverly sneaking off partway through. But she imagined that, among crowds of people, all engaged in meaningless small talk, she could slip away unnoticed by Elijah, who was sure to be busy.

Beverly looked down at her low, black heels and tried to calm her whirring thoughts before the gala. She'd chosen a ruby-red dress with a high neckline, her curly hair tied in a low ponytail. There wasn't even a faint chance that she'd truly fit in with the socialites at the gala, but she was planning to at least look the part—for Elijah, if no one else.

Beverly's bed transformed into her 'prop table': black jeans, a soft, red shirt with a white Peter Pan collar, and her best sneakers laid out before her. She paced around the room, madly in thought. She left the window open, cast the screen aside and hid it in the closet. As Beverly left her room and listened to the sound of her heels tapping on the hardwood stairs, she was fully aware that she was performing as two different characters today, and was determined to be convincing in both roles.

After meeting Daniel downstairs, Beverly climbed into the passenger side of his truck. It was a chilly evening, so she'd brought a thick jacket. Daniel got into the truck after her, wearing his best suit, the same he had worn for the first visit to the Evans Estate but with a different tie this time.

"You know," he started, "I still don't get why you insist on coming with me tonight."

"I told you, Daniel, I was invited."

Daniel shot her a look of disbelief.

"And, how exactly did you get an invitation?"

"Elijah told me I could come. He asked me to."

"Oh, really? We haven't been here two weeks and you've already got an admirer?"

Beverly laughed nervously. "I don't know about that, it was just a casual invite."

"Oh, I see." Daniel put the car in drive. "I guess I just didn't know people got ready for two hours for a *casual* invitation." Daniel gave Beverly a teasing smirk that let her know he was only kidding.

She defended herself. "I'm being serious!"

"Of course you are," Daniel said, pulling out of the driveway. "I guess I'm just impressed that you're going to one of these things voluntarily. They freak me out."

It was only a short drive across town to the Evans's grand house atop a hill, but the place still felt worlds away. Daniel gulped, walking around the perimeter of the truck to let his niece out. She thanked him, and they made their way inside, the cold fall air nipping at Beverly with only black tights covering her shaky legs.

The interior of the Evans Estate today was different from the first time they had ventured inside. On that first day, the near-empty house was full of uncomfortable silence. Now, the place was filled with the steady buzz of conversation and the sound of high heels clicking on the marble floor.

A chandelier hung in the centre of a large, open room to Beverly's right. Her phone was tucked safely in a grey clutch she held defensively close to her side. She didn't own a wristwatch, so she relied on her phone to tell her what time she had to disappear and make her way to Christopher's party. *Twenty-eight minutes,* she thought to herself.

Unlike Daniel and Beverly's first trip to the Evans's home, no one was there to guide them around. They stood next to each other, looking around the house, not comfortable enough to speak to anyone else. She scanned the brightly lit room to the right. Beverly estimated that sixty people graced the ballroom, probably the subset of town members who could afford to dress up for an event such as this, Evans Estate employees, surely. Waiters buzzed around, carrying trays. This seemed to be the heart of the party. Daniel led

Beverly into the ballroom, unsure of where to go or what to do with his hands.

The town mayor, Ms. Rowan, stood near the back of the ballroom, holding a glass of champagne. She was surrounded by three distinguished-looking guests of the Evans family, likely potential investors, holding champagne glasses and chatting with each other. Elijah's parents had dispersed themselves among the guests, appearing to converse strategically. Mrs. Evans, all clad in black and white and pearls, stood on the other end of the ballroom, smiling and talking with a group of men. Mr. Evans had the majority of servers gravitating toward him, as he made polite conversation with a few business people. Elijah was nowhere to be found.

A man in a black suit came toward Beverly and her uncle, offering hors d'oeuvres on a tray. Daniel stepped forward, picking from the many types of food he was offered. Beverly remembered that Milhaven had a curfew approaching, but she supposed that curfew didn't matter for this house. She took her phone out from her clutch and kept it in her hand, so that she could use it to record conversations or take pictures if she noticed anything suspicious.

Beverly caught sight of Elijah from across the room. He was smiling, speaking to a group of men, some of whom appeared to be almost a decade older than him. He, like those surrounding him, was holding a champagne glass, taking sips between laughs and witty anecdotes. One man laughed at something Elijah had said, touching his arm with a strange sense of camaraderie. As Elijah smiled and returned the gesture, he caught Beverly's eyes from across the room. He said something to the men that must have been a goodbye, because he left the group and cut his way through the room.

Seeing Elijah now was different than the first day Beverly had met him. He was wearing a dress shirt with no jacket or tie a week ago, but today he was wearing a sharp black suit, finished off with a bow tie. Everything about him was neat and clean, with the exception of his untamed dark curls.

"You look wonderful tonight, Beverly."

"Thank you," she replied politely. The group of men that Elijah abandoned had turned around, studying Beverly. She noticed their interest in her and looked right back at them. "Are you going to introduce me to your friends?"

"Actually," he said. "I had other plans for tonight. Follow me."

Beverly's eyebrows raised.

With a guiding hand holding her free wrist, Elijah led her out of the ballroom. Beverly didn't know if they were leaving the house, joining another part of the gala, or going somewhere more private, but she followed him anyway.

He led her up a set of staircases. The steps were steep and made of marble, with elegant wooden handrails leading them upstairs. By the sheer height of the building, she estimated that there must have been four, maybe five floors to this house. Beverly lost track of how many staircases she'd climbed.

"I really appreciate you coming here with me. I wouldn't have survived this gala without you," said Elijah.

Beverly was taken aback slightly but didn't stop climbing stairs. "You seemed to be handling yourself just fine before I arrived."

"Well, yes, but it wasn't any fun."

They made a few more turns onto a landing, then he stopped in his tracks. He stood in front of a wall, a normal-looking wall, with paintings and portraits and a very large window covered with curtains. Beverly took a second to catch her breath and caught a look at her phone to check the time.

"Are you ready?" he asked with a smile.

"Ready for what?"

Elijah closed his eyes and chuckled to himself in a way that Beverly found confusing and endearing at the same time. He stepped forward, opened the curtains, and carefully unclasped a latch on the bottom corner of the window, pressing his other hand on the glass. With a creak, the window swung open. Beverly stepped forward, looking out of the window to see what Elijah wanted to show her. She placed both hands on the low windowsill and saw the night sky stretch out in front of her. She could see for miles, far beyond the silhouettes of townhomes and buildings casting shadows on the beautiful landscape.

She smiled. "Why did you take me up here?" Beverly asked.

He looked closer at her. "There's something I need to show you. Just trust me."

Elijah stepped over the windowsill, jumping a foot or so down to a ledge below. Despite the fact that the ledge had hovered sixteen inches away from his feet and falling would result in a swift death, he moved without falter. He turned ninety degrees and disappeared off in a confident stride, not waiting for Beverly.

Beverly's shoulders tensed. She considered going back downstairs, disappearing into the crowd of people, but she couldn't. Elijah was her best shot at making it home, getting back to Mara. If she didn't have this way out, she'd have no future. She slipped off her high heels, leaving them in the middle of the hallway. She placed her hands on the windowsill and tossed her legs over the side, her cold feet absorbing the impact of the jump. She took a moment to steady herself. The ledge was about three feet wide—wide enough for her to walk across, but not a lot of room for error—certainly too narrow for her own comfort.

She held her breath as she inched along the ledge. Her dress scraped against the side of the brick building, coating its skirt with dirt and tendrils of ivy. After a fifteen-foot-long stretch, Beverly saw Elijah sitting on the roof. She smiled as the sun set behind him, and he smiled back.

Beverly climbed up to meet him, glad to be somewhere with less imminent risk of falling to her death. Elijah was leaning back comfortably with his hands resting on the roof behind him. Beverly looked down, noticing the stained skirt of her once pristine dress.

"My dress!" she cried. I'll—"

"Never have to wear it again," Elijah interjected with a sideways smile. "Not where we're going, not if you don't want to."

Beverly took a seat next to him. She could see the entire town from up there. It was small, with every bit of it laid out before her eyes. But the town was dark. That was something she found strange about

Milhaven. Most of the lights in the buildings and homes were out, even when people were not allowed to roam the streets past eleven at night. Beverly would be an exception to that rule tonight.

"I can't wait until we're gone," he began. "We could be out of this tiny, boring town in a number of days, and you will never have to think about this place or the people in it ever again. Don't you want that?"

"Of course," said Beverly, quickly, making Elijah smile. "I can't wait to get out of this place, into the city."

"You have no idea how happy that makes me to hear," Elijah said slowly.

Beverly detected a strange sense of solemnity in his voice.

"More than anything, though," said Beverly, thinking out loud, "I just can't stand thinking about Daniel … having to be stuck here, taking care of me, instead of making a life for himself. I mean, he's in his twenties, for goodness sake, he should be living his life, not taking on a kid."

"Well, he'll be free when we run away," said Elijah. "But, you can't only think about him. You've got to think about yourself as well."

"I know," Beverly said automatically.

"No, I'm serious," said Elijah. "You've got to do this for *you*. I think you've really got a future away from this town. I think … *we* have a future."

Elijah's voice softened as he spoke, leaning into Beverly slightly.

Though she was compelled by Elijah's every word, her mind was preoccupied. She didn't think she could learn anything from talking to him. Beverly needed a reason to leave the gala, to make it to Christopher's party. She needed to go to Christopher's party.

"So, where are we going to go first?" she asked, changing the subject. Elijah looked surprised and a little bit let down, but he continued nonetheless.

"Our first stop? The mines."

Though Beverly asked the question out of casual curiosity, that was not the answer she expected.

"Why would we go to the mines?"

He looked up to her. "To end at the beginning. I've hated every day of living in this town ... I want us to leave it the way it started."

Something about that answer concerned Beverly as those last words rattled around in her brain. She assumed it was important for him, some sort of poetic justice on his part that he'd been thinking about since long before he ever met her. Elijah looked down at her bare feet balanced on the rooftop.

"Oh!" Beverly exclaimed, with a little too much enthusiasm, before correcting herself. "I just forgot. I left my heels in the middle of the hallway. That might look suspicious, I'll go grab them. I'll be right back."

Elijah drew out a long breath, studying Beverly. "Alright."

Beverly turned quickly and did not look back. She crawled back down the roof the same way she left it, made her way across the ledge, and shimmied back through the window.

She stopped for a few long moments, looking back out the window. Why was she so eager to leave? It was just a high school party out there for her, and there was a boy who really cared about her, right here, who was willing to give her absolutely everything she wanted. Even so, she needed to be at this party. Daniel wouldn't take her warning seriously if she didn't have proof that Milhaven had a dark side, that the Evans family wasn't who they said they were. Beverly promised herself she'd find proof. She decided that she'd make up some excuse that Elijah would accept as to why she didn't come back.

She gripped one heel in each hand, trying to make her way down the steps without a sound, knowing that noise echoed in that enormous space. She slipped her shoes back on in an effort to look more presentable before she reached the main floor, but it didn't change the fact that her dress was still stained with grime.

She did her best to cover the stains with her clutch and escaped out the main entrance. Luckily, she didn't see Daniel anywhere, and Elijah was all the way up on the roof, so there was no way she'd be caught.

Beverly realized, after opening the heavy door, that Elijah was still sitting on the roof, peering down. She tried to remember how much of the land beneath the house was visible from the roof. This was assuming, of course, that Elijah was still up there and had not gone looking for her. Beverly decided she just had to be quick. She took a left off the stairs, hugging the side of the building, doing her best to move quickly and stay out of sight.

Beverly noticed how thick the forest was behind the Evans Estate, a dense wood that seemed to go on forever. Staying close to the tree line, she walked all the way down the path and back onto the street.

It was only when Beverly's heart stopped racing that she wondered why she put herself through that escape. She was just so afraid of disappointing Elijah. What was she going to tell him now? As she walked home to get changed for the next party, she started planning her excuse: maybe say she was in the hallway and someone noticed her, asked what she was doing up on that floor; maybe say she was forced to leave; or maybe say Daniel texted her and said there was an emergency—but then what would the emergency be? She kept rehearsing different ideas, but every story seemed to have holes. She promised herself that she'd have a good excuse fabricated before the night was over.

9

Something Beverly always loved about the city was the fact that it never slept. Twenty-four hours a day it was awake and living, but as Beverly strolled home through Milhaven's maze of dark streets, she felt like she was in a ghost town. It wasn't even curfew yet, and the place was nearly dormant. Beverly had assumed that towns with curfews weren't actually asleep by the time curfew came, that there would still be people out stargazing, men out drinking in backyards. There was few signs of life anywhere, hardly even a bedroom light left on. Most of the people seemed to retire for the night as soon as curfew hit. Beverly couldn't imagine how people lived like that.

It was fifteen minutes before curfew when she got to her room to exchange the stained dress and heels for more comfortable clothes. She laced up her sneakers and went right back outside, cutting across the lawn to Christopher's house. Of all the houses on the street, his stood out from the rest. Christopher's house, which was right next to Daniel's, had dim lights shining out through parted curtains and muffled music radiating from its walls. She was glad to be heading toward the only house on the street that showed proof of life inside. Would its quiet music be an invitation for trouble?

Beverly opened the house's unlocked door and stepped inside, scanning the room for familiar faces. This was also a house owned by the Evans family for their employees. The layout of the interior was the same as Daniel's house, as well as the light fixtures and the furniture, but there was none of the cold emptiness that plagued the house she was staying in. If it was the same house as hers, how could it be so entirely different?

The place was full of teenagers, talking and dancing and forming their own little circles around the living room and kitchen table. There were speakers around the house, all playing the same song with a thick bass line. Half-empty glasses and cans were strewn across the tables, the floor, the counter. Unlike Daniel's nearly bare house, the walls here were adorned with picture frames, family photographs, even artwork. This house wasn't even remotely like the one she lived in next door. This was a home.

Beverly found that no one had really noticed her as she walked through the house, not even Christopher, who was pouring drinks behind the kitchen counter. Caroline was nowhere to be found. Beverly wandered toward the kitchen area, hoping to casually get some water or find a bowl of chips to stand next to and not look suspicious. Ideally, tonight would be a night of quietly gathering information.

She looked around, wondering where to go. What group of kids would be most likely to reveal the secrets of this town, and what type of evidence should she be looking for? Just as she was scoping out the best groups to eavesdrop on, a familiar face popped out of nowhere.

"Beverly!" called Simon, with a hint of surprise in his voice.

Beverly just nodded her head in reply.

"I didn't know you were going to be here. Since you left the other day … I didn't mean to make you uncomfortable or anything."

"No, I had a great time," she assured.

"Really?" Simon asked, failing to hide his shock and excitement. He looked back at a group of teenagers on the couch behind him. "I'm glad to hear that."

"Well, I've never been to a poetry reading before."

Simon smiled. "Y'know, Caroline told me that she met you at the parent-teacher social. Why'd you go if you won't be in town long?"

Beverly took in a sharp breath. She should never have told this boy the truth. "Well, I'm enrolled, but I'm only going to be here for a couple of months, so—"

"Months? Oh! I thought this was a quick visit, I didn't realize you had so much time. So, where are you staying?"

Beverly didn't know if she should keep this conversation going. Simon was truly being kind by trying to be her friend, but she just couldn't handle it. She was too afraid of slipping into a comfortable rhythm, making friends, connections, planning a future in Milhaven. She knew that people didn't leave Milhaven easily, especially not if they stayed for too long. Any reason she had to live in this town was a reason to die in it, and Beverly refused to die in a town like Milhaven. It would be just like dying alone.

"I live with my uncle right now. Daniel."

"Daniel? Right, doesn't he work for the Evans?"

"Looks that way."

"I knew he was moving into the neighbourhood, but I didn't know you were his niece," Simon said.

"Yeah, well," she replied, "it's an awfully small town, you would've found out eventually."

He chuckled a bit. "It might be small, but it's not so awful."

"Well ..."

"No, really. It's nowhere near as bad as it seems." He defended the town cheerfully.

"Oh, I wasn't trying to be insulting or anything," Beverly backpedaled. "I've hardly seen it. I just heard a few things about it being ... not the greatest place to live."

"Maybe not for everyone, that's true. I wouldn't be too quick to pass judgment, though. Besides, a town can't really be good or bad. Anything so human has to be more complex than just good or bad."

Beverly didn't know what to say to that. She just quietly agreed.

"I can show you the beautiful parts of Milhaven if you want, like

Stephen's house—the parts I love. And, I promise, nights at that house are usually so much better than that terrible poetry."

Beverly couldn't help but smile. What a beautiful offer.

"That sounds great, I'm just not really looking for connections at this point."

"Right, because you and your uncle, you're leaving soon?"

"No, um. He'll be staying."

"So, what about you, where will you go?" Simon asked.

"I don't know."

Simon's face scrunched up for a fraction of a second. "You're not planning on running away, are you?"

Beverly's eyebrow raised. "Well, I don't know if you could call it that, I'm more like … switching guardians. I just need to get out of town."

"That's not a good idea," Simon said, speeding through the words.

"What do you mean?"

"Just that, with your uncle, um," he said, "it's a bad idea to run away from Milhaven."

"Why can't I?" Beverly pressed. Perhaps she would find the evidence she needed tonight after all, or at least a lead.

Simon looked as though he didn't know what to say. "Well, you've hardly even seen anything here yet."

A disappointing answer. The boy obviously didn't want her to stay in Milhaven for sightseeing—something else was going on. She needed answers. She needed to guide this conversation toward the secrets of the town, anything that could lead her to any sort of hard proof.

"I think a couple of weeks is enough to see what I need to."

Beverly's gaze wandered over to the living room, where she saw another familiar face. The boy from school, the one who almost hit her with his car, the one who talked to her in the gym, Luke. He looked different now. He had a dark jacket on and thick boots that left marks on Christopher's floor. He faced a group of kids—most appeared younger than he was, each of them hanging on his every word.

"It's ..." Simon started, then looked behind him. He could tell that Beverly's attention had been drawn elsewhere.

Beverly and Simon could hear Luke speaking from across the room.

"Yeah, no joke, three hundred dollars for one day's work. No longer than a school day, really, and it's just forty-five minutes away from town. Moving around some supplies, no strings, no questions asked."

The small crowd that Luke was propositioning responded with a murmur of consideration. Beverly watched from a distance, then realized that she wasn't the only one listening in. Half the heads in the room had turned toward him.

"Hey!" Christopher shouted from across the room, with a sharp tone that Beverly hadn't expected him to be capable of. He walked toward the living room. "You can't do that here. Take your business outside."

Beverly never thought she'd ever see Christopher angry, not the boy she'd seen quietly reading poetry about love. Luke didn't seem discouraged by Christopher's warning. Everyone in the room fell silent, only the music broke the hush. Another boy, one of the kids that had been listening to him preach, stepped forward. Beverly held her breath.

"Hey, this doesn't have anything to do with you, stay out of it." The boy was standing straight and tall, tightening a fist and choosing words that made him sound tough. He was forgetting that eyes speak as well. His fear overshadowed his words.

Luke found great amusement in this. "Yeah, Chris, stay out of it." He chuckled and patted him on the shoulder.

"I said you can't run that in here, Luke," Christopher said firmly.

Luke threw a punch at Christopher, sending everyone else in the room back a few steps in shock. Christopher took the blow, cradling his jaw in his hands. He straightened up and barreled forward to throw himself at Luke. The kids surrounding both the boys began closing in on the fight, and Beverly couldn't see what was happening to Christopher anymore. Suddenly, everyone around them was pushing, shoving, just one mass of bodies, some of them attempting to protect each one of the boys, others struggling to leave the house. Beverly sprang forward, shouldering through the crowd, trying to get through the mass of teenagers, when a hand tightened around her wrist.

Amid the chaos, Beverly turned her head sharply to see who had grabbed her. It was Simon. Beverly's first instinct was to rip her arm away, get to safety. She tried to speak but her thoughts were being drowned out by the music and the rumble of the fight. Simon tried to lead her around the perimeter of the room and toward the door.

"Let me go! Aren't you going to help him?" Beverly shouted through the noise, her voice cracking.

Reaching the other side of the room, Simon ripped open the front door and swept Beverly outside. Once they were out, he immediately slammed the door shut, and the noise abruptly disappeared.

"You need to get out of here," Simon said.

"But he's your friend! Aren't you going to help him?" she hissed.

"Chris will be fine, I'll make sure of it, don't worry. He can take care of himself."

"Don't worry? What are you talking about?"

"You should get home. And Beverly, just … don't run away. It's not a good idea." Simon's eyes were pleading.

The front door flew open again and out came Luke, emerging from the fight unscathed. He turned up the collar of his heavy jacket, shot Beverly a sideways glance, and made his way down the road. Beverly felt like she should do or say something to Luke, but she stood in silence as a flood of teenagers poured out the main entrance. Beverly had never seen people scatter so fast. She found herself lost in the crowd until Simon pulled her aside.

"Please, just get home, okay? As quickly as you can."

Simon stepped backward onto the grass, looking all around, terrified. He swallowed, turned, and made his way back inside the house.

Beverly decided that she couldn't go back inside. Not knowing what else to do, she started walking, rushing home and up to her bedroom. She felt so defeated. She wasn't any closer to finding evidence for Daniel than she was before. Beverly spent that night solemnly gazing out of her bedroom window. She couldn't help but think that Elijah was still on that rooftop watching over her, looking down mournfully as the lights of the town went dark, one by one, like falling stars.

everly had always loved the city. She moved around so often that when she was really young, she felt as though she were being raised in all the cities of the world.

Before she landed in the foster care system, Beverly travelled far and wide with her parents. The more places she saw, the more in love she fell with city life. She used to drag her parents from cafés to toy stores, gawking at the tall buildings, watching the lights reflecting off the lakes, and studying the views from hotel room windows. More than anything, she loved the quiet nights, taking long car rides with both her parents in the front seats. They used to bicker with each other, but, being so young, Beverly never quite understood what they were arguing about. She used to sit in the back seat with an open book in her hands, riding over great bridges and over greater lakes, catching glimpses of sentences beneath the passing streetlights.

Beverly found herself feeling more and more distant from those memories every day she spent in Milhaven. That scared her. The memories she had of her parents and with Mara, they were the only things getting her through this small-town life. More importantly, they were giving her the strength to leave.

On a misty November afternoon, the day after the party, Beverly sat outside her house because she'd been instructed to. A note she had found on her front door that morning, signed by Elijah, told her to wait outside for him, that they needed to talk. He had already demonstrated that he was capable of climbing up to reach her window when he wanted to see her, but something was different about this instance. Beverly was shocked by how invasive it felt that he came to her house when she was asleep, not just to see her but to demand something from her. She sat on the patio with her elbows pressing into her knees, her eyes trained on the white-painted wood, waiting for Elijah to show up. She felt as though she had been called into the principal's office.

When Elijah stormed through the space between her house and the fence, it was easy to see that something was wrong.

"Why would you do it?" His tone was demanding. It was a simple question, but Beverly didn't have an answer. "Why would you run away from me? For some party?" Anger cut through his words.

Beverly wondered if she could give him a rational reason for her choice to trade in a night with him for a high school party. But he didn't seem to be looking for an excuse. He was looking for an apology—that, or the satisfaction of hearing her admit to the mistake.

"Look, Eli, I was just ..." she trailed off and couldn't decide whether or not she owed him the apology he believed he deserved.

"I offered you everything. Everything! I offered you a free ride out of this hellhole, and you just run away from me? God, you have to trust me, Beverly. How the hell are we supposed to start a new life together if you can't even do that?"

"You're right. You're absolutely right, I shouldn't have left. I'm so sorry."

Elijah let out a breath, his eyes narrowing in on her. "How did you even find out about the party, anyway?" Elijah asked.

"Christopher's girlfriend asked me after school one day. I'm the new kid, she was just being nice."

"I know about what happened at the party. That kid Christopher, he's not your friend. He shouldn't have confronted Luke, he should have just let them do their thing. Bad things happen to people who interfere with my parents' business, Bev. That's why we've got to leave, this stuff's been happening forever, this whole town's going straight to hell."

She thought for a moment. "If this town's going to hell, why are you still here?" Beverly asked, not knowing whether or not it was in her best interest to do so.

Elijah took a deep breath and shook his head. "Because you're here, Bev. I'm not leaving without you."

"Why?" she asked, believing it was a fair question.

"I've already told you. It's because you're different. You don't belong in a place like this. I don't know why you went to that kid's party last night, but sooner or later you've got to learn to take my advice. Do *not* make this town your home. It's too dangerous. I don't want you ending up like your friend Christopher."

Elijah's words rang in Beverly's head as he turned to leave. *What did that mean? Was Christopher in trouble?* She fought to speak, to say something, to call out anything that matched the thoughts that were boiling in her head, but she didn't have the words. Her first-class ticket to a new life was walking off her driveway. She betrayed him, and yet, he still wanted to take her with him. She couldn't understand why Elijah would want her to go with him, but she was glad he did, or she'd be stuck in that awful little town forever.

She spent the rest of the weekend inside her house, until Monday morning came.

Unafraid of being late for school, she stopped by the post office and accepted her third letter from Mara. She ran straight home with the letter clutched in her hand. Beverly stole away to her room, through the empty house, so she could read the letter on her bed. The letters that Mara sent were always very short. Ever since ALS had begun leeching her muscle strength, she did all of her writing on the computer, but typing was still challenging. Mara hated the fact that writing was so difficult for her, but Beverly knew that because of it, every word she sent was filled with meaning:

Beverly,

I'm glad to hear about the inspiration you derive from your new home.

> *I'd love to see what you've painted someday. Milhaven sounds like such a beautiful place from the way you've described it.*
>
> *As long as you keep an open mind about Daniel, I'm sure you'll do just fine with your new life.*
>
> *Love,*
>
> *Mara*

Beverly looked down at the letter and the envelope it was held in. Mara always sprayed her letters with her favourite lavender-scented perfume, but Beverly didn't want to smell it right now. The thought of Mara labouring to respond to her lies made her feel sick. She put the letter in her closet, with the other ones. She hadn't even started the paintings that she told Mara she'd done, of the beautiful scenery and small-town beauty of Milhaven. After Elijah criticized her for putting the paintings up in her room, she'd packed her art supplies back up and put them away.

After wandering around the house for a little while, Beverly decided that she might as well get to school. She walked back to Milhaven High, thinking about what she might have painted if she had allowed herself.

Beverly made it to school in time for second period. She spent the day trudging between classrooms, each class bleeding into the next. It felt as though someone shook her awake in the middle of the day when, just before class was meant to end, an announcement came over the PA. Beverly was called to see the guidance counsellor. She gathered her books and found her way to Mr. Matthews's room, hesitantly tapping on the door.

The door wasn't completely shut. The guidance counsellor, Mr. Matthews, had an 'open-door policy,' but today that door was just left ajar. He was younger than any of the other teachers and had a knack for fading into the background at school events. He opened up the door, asking her to come in and take a seat. More than anything, Beverly wanted to know why she'd been called in for a meeting in the first place, but she didn't want to go ahead and ask him, fearing something was very wrong.

"So, Beverly, I just wanted to make sure you're doing all right with your classes so far," Mr. Matthews said plainly.

"Everything's fine," she assured him, knowing that Mr. Matthews was likely to press her further.

"I've been told that you might be having some trouble integrating into our little community here. You haven't been engaged in classes, you didn't stay for the parent-teacher social, or come to our talent show. Nobody saw you this morning. Is everything okay?"

Beverly realized, all in one moment, that her actions reflected on Daniel just as much as they did on her. The way she acted, how she behaved in school, whether or not she showed up, it would all be perceived as a reflection of Daniel's guardianship.

"Yes, sorry, there isn't anything wrong. Are people worried about me?" She thought it was better to follow up her reply with a question, to turn the conversation back on him.

"Well, some people were wondering if you're having a hard time adjusting. I wonder, though, if you even want to adjust."

Beverly's eyes widened, and she suddenly felt very vulnerable. Mr. Matthews didn't seem to be confrontational, or aggressive in nature, just curious, concerned. Beverly was tempted to say 'I'm sorry sir, I'm not sure what you mean,' but Mr. Matthews would have seen through the act. His kind eyes and nurturing demeanor let Beverly know she would be safe in her honesty.

"Well, admittedly, sir, I don't plan on living here for very long," she said.

"That's okay," said Mr. Matthews, to Beverly's surprise. "I know you're just in high school now, you're young. You might want to move away as soon as you're able to, and that's okay. Just think of your time in this new town as a chapter in your life. It doesn't have to be long, if that's your choice, but either way, it's still an important part of your story."

Beverly nodded, processing his advice.

He spoke again. "I know that you're probably going to want to leave for college or work, and I know there's a big world out there for you, but please don't discount the merits of this town just because it's small. We're part of that world, too."

Beverly looked confused for a moment. She had never heard such sincere advice from a guidance counsellor, or met one that cared so much. Elijah had said that Milhaven was dangerous, but how could that be true if people like Mr. Matthews, like Simon, like Caroline, believed in it so strongly? Beverly began to reconsider her outlook on Milhaven and of the people there.

"Okay," said Beverly, looking down at her feet. "I'll think about that." It ended the conversation, but Mr. Matthews understood that it wasn't dismissive. She really was going to think about it. Beverly thanked him, assured him that she'd participate in her classes, and went out into the hallway.

On her way to dump her books in her locker, Beverly watched Simon jog through the halls to catch up with her.

"Hey! Beverly!" he called out. "Look ... I'm really sorry about the party. It shouldn't have gone down the way it did. And I'm sorry I was so abrupt, and um, secretive. I promise, I'll tell you everything you want to know. Maybe you could meet me, tonight, at Rosie's, say at five-thirty?"

The honesty in his voice was transparent. Beverly had not received an apology quite so sincere in a very long time. 'I'll tell you everything' was a tempting offer, and she completely believed he would. She was beyond curious about the strange and disconcerting goings-on of the town, the things Elijah would only discuss with a vague lack of detail. This invitation seemed to carry a lot of weight.

"Yeah. Yeah, I'll see you there."

A smile gleamed on Simon's face. "Okay. Yeah, okay, I'll see you then." Simon turned into the steady flow of teenagers heading to their next class, pulling him away from her. He looked back at Beverly as he made his way back through the school. "That's a promise!" he called out, unaware or uncaring of all the other kids around that heard. Beverly couldn't stop a smile from creeping onto her face, as she turned and let the mass of students rushing out of the school lead her out with them. *Finally,* she thought. *A promise I can keep.*

Elijah was standing next to his car, which was parked haphazardly beside the school. He was facing away from the school's entrance, his cell phone pressed to his ear.

"No, Doug, this is your problem," Elijah spat out, with a sharp edge to his words. "No, obviously I had nothing to do with … Doug, we're talking about eighty thousand dollars, do you really think I would take that?"

He started to pace while he spoke, but never turned around or spotted Beverly, who was pressing her back against the side of the school, trying to look as though she wasn't listening. She could easily make out everything he was saying, and his jagged tone of voice indicated that he meant every word of it.

"Well, you're a smart man, Doug. I'm positive that you'll find a way to make up the difference if you don't want my parents to find out," Elijah taunted. He placed one hand on the side of his car and leaned onto it, turning ever so slightly, as Beverly cautiously took a couple of steps toward him.

"*Figure it out*. Don't call me about this again," Elijah spat into his phone, before hanging up and throwing it onto the seat of his car.

Beverly stood still for a few measured seconds so Elijah wouldn't think she had been eavesdropping on the disturbing conversation. She then walked toward him, to the street that would take her home, wondering if Elijah would say anything to her as she passed.

He caught sight of her and called out her name, gesturing for her to come over to his car.

"We're going," he said. "We're getting out of town right now. Get in the car."

Beverly stood in her room, clutching her backpack to her chest. Elijah's instructions played over and over in her head. *Pack your bag, you're not coming back.* She was told to pack light: just some clothes, some food, a few bottles of water, a sleeping bag, a backpack, and whatever else she needed for a weekend-long trip; just enough to tide them over until they could buy what they needed. He was parked on the street outside her house, impatiently waiting for her to finish packing and join him. She had run away from home more than once, but something felt wrong this time. Wasn't this exactly what she wanted?

Beverly looked down at her floor. Laid out in front of her was a bundle of shirts, sweaters, socks, and jeans. She knew she had no time to sort through it, so she stuffed it all into her backpack and zipped it up. She looked at her closet of art supplies, old paintings. She left it all behind and ran down the stairs. She needed water, so she quickly foraged through the kitchen's cupboards for water bottles.

Beverly could feel Elijah's presence outside as she stood in her own kitchen. She felt like he was watching her, somehow, through the windows or the crack in the doorframe. She wondered if he was going to jump out from behind the fridge or from under the stairs, just to catch her in a lie or to tell her to go faster, that she didn't have all day, that someone would notice them escaping if she wasn't ready soon. She heard a car horn go off twice—two short warnings from Elijah to hurry up.

She quickly threw open every single cabinet door in the kitchen, scanning each one for a bottle, or bottles, big enough to sustain her for a day or two. She found lots of dishes and glasses, but not any bottles. She reached for the knobs on one of the last cupboards in the kitchen, one that towered above her head. A slip of her hand caused a white dish to fall out, topple over, and crash to the floor.

"Sorry!" Beverly blurted out loud, not even realizing she had done it. The bowl, she found out quickly, was just plastic and hadn't shattered. Her unconscious apology worried her. She was afraid of how on edge she was, of the way her hands were fumbling despite the careful work they were able to do with paint. Choking down her fear, she checked the fridge for water bottles. There were some there, so she threw two into the bottom of her bag. She was about to make her way to the door when she turned around to look at what she'd done to the kitchen.

Every cupboard door was left open, the counter left a mess, a white bowl lying upside down in the middle of the floor. It was a haunting sight to see the room like that. It was something a ghost might do—the kind that tries to communicate their existence to the living, that they're still around and stuck in the home they died in. It crushed her to know that Daniel would come home to find this. Unable to look back, Beverly left the house.

She walked around to the right side of the car and climbed into the passenger seat.

"Hey," she said, with a semi-cheerful tone.

"Hey."

"You, um," she proceeded, "you looked like you were calling someone after school today. Looked pretty heated." She was testing the waters for what she presumed to be a very long drive.

"Oh, parents," he said, flatly.

He started driving, never taking his eyes off the road. His mouth rested in a harsh, flat line.

"I'm sorry," she said. It was the only thing she could think to say.

"I just—" Elijah let anger slip into his voice as he tightened his grip on the steering wheel and swerved the car. For a fraction of a second, Beverly worried they were going to crash.

Elijah gathered himself. "I'm so done with their controlling bull-shit. I'm not getting involved in their family business. They might own this town, but not me, I'm not a part of it anymore." The change of tone in his voice surprised Beverly. It was less aggressive, almost quiet. "And you aren't either," he finished, with sincerity. His words were more measured and his driving became less erratic. She found relief in this.

Elijah slumped his shoulders forward. Beverly switched on the radio and turned the volume way up. They drove like that for forty-five minutes.

They spent the rest of the drive in comfortable silence, and when they did speak, it was about nothing important. Beverly directed most of her attention out the window with a hesitant goodbye to the town of Milhaven. As they were leaving the town, she watched it blend into forest, then to thicker forest, then to open valleys, until even the valleys were behind them. The mining site was just up ahead.

They drove down a grassy pathway and the mining property opened up before them. There wasn't much to see, other than mounds of dirt or gravel, and the scattered dilapidated building. Beverly imagined that the site smelled like dust, dirt and peeled paint. She noticed heaps of jagged metal from what was likely decommissioned machinery off in the distance, as well as pieces of caution tape littered around the site's perimeter.

"Finally," Elijah exhaled.

He looked over to Beverly, a quiet signal that told her to get out of the car. Elijah walked around to the back of the car and opened the trunk. It was only then when Beverly realized how much he had packed in comparison to her. In the trunk was a sleeping bag, a pack of water bottles, boxes of food, a stretch of rope coiled into a loop, and two extra backpacks. Elijah's packing was meticulous and intentional, to fit as much as he could in a relatively small space. But even with all of this comfortingly elaborate preparation, Beverly knew that this would not sustain two people for very long.

Beverly threw her backpack over her shoulder and trudged forward. A bright-yellow 'Keep Out' sign guarded the site and blocked their way. Shredded caution tape littered the ground around the sign.

"Are we just going to take a quick look around or …?" Beverly's question trailed off as she turned up the collar of her jacket and stepped over the low-hanging rope that tried to act as a perimeter fence.

She had no idea what a mine site was supposed to look like, but she wasn't impressed. It was just splintered structures, the dusty roads that connected them, and caves casting grey shadows onto the rocky ground. She found it difficult to believe that Elijah wanted to stay for even a short time in a place this drab.

"Over there." Elijah pointed toward a wooden building that wasn't too far from the car.

He had already set out for the structure, his backpack slung over his shoulder and his hiking boots untied. Beverly jogged to catch up with him.

The wooden structure could best be described as a shack. Only about a third of the ceiling remained, most of it was gone. Wooden boards were nailed together overhead, the floor covered with dirt and cobwebs. This was somewhere for people to take shelter for a short time, but not a place anyone could live.

"Why are we here?" Beverly asked.

"It could be useful. It's sheltered enough if we plan on staying the night."

He dumped his book bag on the ground and walked out through an empty door frame.

"Staying the night?" Beverly asked. She couldn't understand why they weren't already on the road, on her way to Mara.

"Yeah," said Elijah. "It's just one night. You're not in any rush, are you?"

It was the kind of thing that would have sounded like a joke if Elijah hadn't said the words with such disinterest.

Why does he want to stay here? It doesn't make any sense, there's nothing here that could possibly be of any interest to him. Beverly thought the reason he wanted to stop at the mines was to spite the place where corrupt employers exploited workers, because of the way he felt exploited by his family—a quick and satisfying metaphor.

Elijah had wandered off. Beverly thought they should get out of town as soon as possible anyway, in case they got caught, or if people thought to look for them.

Beverly checked her phone. There were two missed calls from Simon.

Simon. Beverly had almost forgotten about Simon. She visualized him sitting at Rosie's alone, waiting for her, and a surge of guilt washed up inside her. She imagined him pacing, calling her over and over again, wondering why she hadn't shown up, wondering if something happened to her. She desperately wanted to know how long Simon had waited there for her, as if it would change anything. Simon was only a short drive back into town, Beverly could make it. He could still be waiting there for her.

"Beverly!" barked Elijah. "Get over here. I want to show you something."

Beverly jumped, scrambling outside to follow his voice. Elijah stood on the other side of the mine site facing the mountain. She followed him toward the mountain, feeling as though she had no other choice. They approached two openings in the mountainside, both about eight feet tall and six feet wide. Beverly peered into the depths of the caves, wondering how long it had been since anyone had dared to enter them. Elijah flicked on his flashlight and pointed it toward the cave on the left.

"You … want me to go in there?" Beverly asked in confused disbelief.

"Well, we're here, aren't we? We might as well take a look."

Elijah gestured for Beverly to go ahead of him, which she did. He was right. They had already come all the way out here, and it would be pointless to turn back now.

It was dark inside the tunnel. The rocky ground felt extremely unsteady underfoot. The flashlight behind her cast a stretched shadow that she followed. As she delved deeper, the previously high cave walls began to sink down, tightening over her head. There were wooden reinforcements overhead, lining the sides of the tunnel, with no signs of decay. The blinding light and quiet footsteps were a constant reminder to Beverly that Elijah was only a short distance behind her.

Beverly's foot slipped. Her ankle twisted under her and she fell forward, catching herself a moment away from hitting the ground. She found her balance again and stood with her arms out and her eyes trained on the darkness before her.

"You alright?" asked Elijah.

"Um," Beverly paused. She felt extremely unsettled, in a way that was hard to describe. She didn't like Elijah's voice behind her, and she didn't like the way her shadow lay distorted on the jagged rocks ahead of her. Her limbs felt stiff. "Yeah, I'm fine."

Elijah said nothing, and they both continued to walk. Once they reached the end of the short tunnel, it forked into two separate paths: the straight path on the left a continuation of the tunnel, and a second path veered off without wooden supports. Elijah turned his flashlight, showing the path on the right. With more light, she could see that the tunnel cut off abruptly. After about twenty feet of rocks and grime, there was a steep drop. A mineshaft, about five feet in diameter, went directly down into the mountain. The bottom of the mineshaft wasn't visible, but there was little doubt that no one could survive a fall from the top.

"I suppose this is as good a place as any," Elijah stated.

Beverly stopped in her tracks, confused and disconcerted by his tone. She was about to turn to him, but she stopped herself. Beverly was determined to wash the fear from her face before she did. Of all the fear and all the discomfort she felt in Milhaven, this was incomparable. Even though she had never questioned Elijah's intentions, being alone with him in the dark was rapidly undermining any trust she did have in him.

She turned to look at him. "Why did you take me here, Elijah?" she asked.

"Because a tragedy is about to take place," he said matter-of-factly. "I'm going to fall down that mineshaft."

"I don't understand," Beverly challenged weakly.

The air, already a little scarce, seemed to thicken around her. The loose stones rolled beneath her feet as the ground began to feel more unsteady.

"I'm going to get a closer look down that mineshaft. I'll walk over to it, get a little too close to the edge and slip on a rock. I'll fall down the mineshaft, never to be seen again. That's our story. Actually, that's your story."

"What are you talking about?" The words came out much quieter, much smaller than Beverly had intended.

"Look I … I'm actually sorry about this," Elijah said. "There's something I've never told you about Milhaven."

"What is it?" asked Beverly, knowing fully well what he was about to say. Stephen's letters were true.

"There's a reason why nobody leaves town. It's because nobody can. My parents aren't just controlling, they're criminal. The town's economy depends on their illegal trade, it's been covered up with murder. We're all guilty. When people leave town … they're a liability to our family. If I ran away from home, I still wouldn't be free from them. There's only one way I can get out of here in a way that no one will find me. I need to fake my death. I need you to help me."

"Fake your death? What are you talking about, we can leave together."

"No, we can't. My parents will find us, they'll drag me back."

"So, I'm just supposed to throw my life away so you can get away from your parents?"

"They'll …" he stopped. "They'll kill Daniel. You have no idea the lengths that my parents will go to, this is really the only way."

"Was this the plan since I got here?" Beverly asked, her voice shaking.

"It…" Elijah sighed. "Yes. This was always the plan. It isn't personal. Even before I met you, Bev, I knew I needed to get away from my parents somehow. It wasn't safe for me, I have so much more life to live, this was the only way—"

"This is not what you promised me," Beverly snapped, tears welling up in her eyes.

"Beverly," said Elijah, "as soon as I'm gone, it'll be like you never knew me, you can go on with life as normal."

"I don't want to do that. You know me, Elijah, you know why I needed to leave. You know why I can't go back."

"I'm sorry. I'm sorry, but this is the only way." He said it as though he were trying to convince himself it was true.

"Shut up," Beverly spat. "You can't do that to me. I won't, I can't go back to Milhaven, and I'm not lying for you."

"Please, Bev, it's what's best. Besides, you're leaving so many people behind. Can you really bear to leave Daniel home alone, working for my parents? Do you know what they'll do to him?"

She felt his tone change all of a sudden. He was no longer trying to be convincing—he was getting angry. Beverly walked down the tunnel, away from the sharp drop, as Elijah followed her.

"Oh, yeah, so now you care about my family, after planning on screwing me over? Don't pretend you care about anyone in this town except yourself, there *are* other ways, you're just selfish."

"Selfish?" Elijah asked viciously. He stepped forward, and Beverly moved away from him, but in the tunnel's darkness, she could hardly tell where her own feet were leading her. "You didn't grow up with them! You have no idea what it's like to have to live with my family, see what they do to people."

Beverly tripped. Something hit her boot, and she stumbled, catching the wall for balance. Her hand collided with the cave wall, and a jagged edge cut her skin.

Elijah's light shone over her feet, revealing a pile of bones scattered across the ground. Beverly scrambled to get away from them with Elijah still cornering her.

"This," said Elijah. "This is what my parents do to people, what I'd have to do if I stayed, you have to understand why you need to do this for—"

Beverly gathered all of her strength and barreled toward him, stepping off her back foot and swinging her fist toward his nose. With all that she had, she threw herself into a punch, her tightened fist hitting Elijah's face an inch or so left of her target. He stumbled back a few steps, holding his face with a cupped hand.

In his other hand, Elijah clutched the flashlight, throwing light around the cave in disorienting strobes. Only a fraction of the day's light twisted around the tunnel corners and lit up the entrance to the cave. Beverly could see Elijah in the small amount of light reflected onto his shadowy frame. Blood gathered on his upper lip, smeared onto his hand; not enough blood to stop him, but certainly enough to make him angry. Elijah raised his gaze to look at Beverly, carrying only cruelty and anger in his stiffened face. He looked down at her with pure contempt. It was the first time that Beverly couldn't find any light at all behind the dark hazels of his eyes. It was like staring down a black hole.

Despite the blood streaming from his nose, Elijah retained his composure. When he found his balance, he moved closer to her, grabbed her shoulder with his bloody fist and spoke again. There was no anger in his voice now, just focus. There was sincerity in his cruelty.

"Look … you're going back to Milhaven. Not because I'm forcing you, but because there's nowhere else for you to go. And, you're going to tell everyone who'll listen that I died today."

He turned and walked back along the path they entered, and this time, Beverly did not follow him.

With Elijah gone and out of sight, the tunnel fell silent. Beverly felt as though she was surrounded by miles of nothing and no one. All she could hear was the muted dripping of water along the tunnel's walls coupled with her own unsteady breath. She took short, shallow hiccups of air as if she was trying to choke down the last remaining gasps of oxygen left in the tunnel.

She wasn't at all aware of time passing, but after a while, she assumed that Elijah had gotten into a car that he must have stashed and made his way off to whatever city or town he'd disappear to. Beverly's stinging eyes focused on the ground in front of her, her gaze drifting from the jagged stones digging into her knees to the end of one of the connecting tunnels.

The shadow of a figure emerged at the front of the cave. Undeniably human, tall, but with a frame too small to be Elijah. Before she had time to think, she scrambled to her feet and ran. Beverly ran blindly, thoughtlessly, down the unknown passageway to her left, her legs taking her places her mind hadn't had the chance to consider yet.

She didn't know which winding tunnel or passageway would lead her to safety, she simply prayed for light at the end of each of the tunnels she barrelled down. She took a left, and a right, and another right. Her vision and her breathing seemed to fail her all at once. She couldn't be sure if either making it to the exit or hiding somewhere deep in the cave would put her at an advantage over her mystery assailant.

She decided that she couldn't run forever, so she tried to do her best to turn back, follow the path toward daylight. She turned one final time, stopping in her tracks and skidding on loose pieces of rock and ash.

It was Simon. He ran forward, seeing Beverly, and then the blood on her hands and sleeves. "Oh, my God, Beverly, are you okay?"

She stood a little taller to meet his eyes, doing her absolute best to prove to him that she really was okay. "I'm fine ..."

"Is this your blood?" he asked, gesturing to her white jacket, stained with the blood she'd wiped from her hands.

"No."

"Elijah's?"

"Yes." Her voice trembled.

"Oh, God," he said. "Come on, we've got to get this off you, quickly."

He pulled the jacket off her shoulders and threw the bloody white fabric to the corner of the tunnel.

"Is he dead?" he asked, with an urgency that Beverly didn't often associate with Simon.

"No."

She wanted to say 'he's alive, and safe, and driving away as fast as he can, escaping with the future he promised he'd share with me.' The words just didn't come out.

"Okay. We need to get you out of here, right now. Please, just come with me, it's all going to be alright. We just need to move fast."

Simon placed one hand on her shoulder, the other on her waist, and led Beverly, with a dazed expression, out of the tunnel and into the light of day. As she emerged into the sunlight, her eyes started stinging. It took time to adjust to the brightness, time she didn't have. Simon urged her forward, trying to get her to run with him toward his car. The blood on Beverly's fingers was even more obvious in the sunlight. A police car swerved around the corner and came to a hard stop, parking perpendicular to them and blocking off the exit road. Simon swore under his breath.

There were two men sitting in the police car: the sheriff, and his deputy on the passenger's side. They both got out of the vehicle at the same time and stormed toward Beverly and Simon.

Beverly was consciously trying to imitate Simon, who looked extremely comfortable, despite the circumstances. He stood tall, maintaining respectable eye contact, not fidgeting with his hands. He was communicating to the officers 'we have done nothing wrong' without even saying a word to them.

"Hey!" the sheriff barked. "What the hell are you two—"

"Not looking for any trouble, sir," Simon cut in. He had absolutely no qualms about cutting off an already visibly upset police officer.

The sheriff had a gun on his hip, and his mouth formed a hard, straight line.

"I'm going to have to ask you both to get in the car," the deputy replied. "We'll take you back to town."

Beverly remembered the words she heard from Elijah just fifteen minutes ago. *You're going back to Milhaven. Not because I'm forcing you, but because you have nowhere else to go.* Her throat tightened, and she choked down half a whimper that could have turned into a sob.

"Are we under arrest, officer?" Simon asked.

"What? No—"

"Then are we free to drive ourselves back?"

The men looked at each other.

"I guess so," the sheriff said, his eyes narrowing. "We'll escort you back to the station."

Simon took Beverly's hand and led her to his car. Beverly's eyes were burning, her throat tight. She climbed into the car, avoiding the stares of the two angry officers. What happened in the darkness of the cave had felt like a bizarre dream. Something about being out in the light of day made everything feel too real, in a way that Beverly couldn't handle.

She gripped the door handle with a tight fist as she fought to control her heavy breathing.

"It's okay," Simon said in his most consoling voice. "Just breathe, Beverly. It's going to be okay."

His words didn't help. Beverly didn't think anybody could help. A quiet tear ran down her cheek.

"We should go," Beverly whispered through a choked breath.

Simon turned the car on and drove out of the lot and back onto the road toward Milhaven.

The drive to the mines had felt as easy as taking a single breath. The road back was long, and every second of it was endured by Beverly fighting for breath.

"Did he hurt you?" Simon asked, turning his gaze away from the road and toward Beverly.

"No."

"So, that's his blood?"

Beverly nodded.

A moment passed.

"How did you know to come get me?" Beverly asked.

"Christopher saw you leave your house with Elijah in a hurry."

"Oh," Beverly said, thinking about how small the chances were of that happening. "I'm really sorry about all this …"

"I wish you wouldn't be. Absolutely none of this is your fault, Beverly."

She didn't have the words to tell him how wrong he was. She knew it was all her fault, allowing herself to get tangled up in Elijah's scheme. Beverly had truly believed that he had all the answers, that he was the only one in the whole town who wasn't brainwashed. How much of that was fake? She thought herself a fool for believing Elijah when he said she was special. His feigned interest in her had been nothing more than a ploy to steal back power from his parents, power she thought he had already inherited a long time ago.

"I guess it just doesn't feel that way."

Beverly realized how naive she had been, to think that Elijah just wanted to take her with him because she was special, different. He needed a way out of town, the same thing Beverly was looking for. She was his leverage.

Once they passed the town's welcome sign, familiar sights began flooding into view. The roads, the graffiti walls, the things Beverly had planned to never see again.

They pulled in to the police station, one of the places in town that Beverly had yet to become familiar with. The station was a long building with chipped brown paint and two front doors. The building sat on a bed of cracked cement. There were no windows, but lights shone through the glass panels in the doors.

Simon pulled up in front of the building, watching the two men in the police car beside them get out at the same time. Much to their surprise, Beverly and Simon weren't handcuffed or even touched, but they were led inside.

The interior of the building was about as uninteresting as the exterior. The front reception area was filled with dull blues and greys, with earthy, wooden flooring. Almost no natural light came into the police station, just a few light bulbs overhead, the light pale and wavering from years of use. The yellow light shone into Beverly's eyes. A single policeman sat at a coffee-stained table with a magazine. With this man, the sheriff, and the deputy, the entirety of the town's police force had congregated, all three of them.

The town was not built for fair trial or incarceration for any length of time, which was evident from the lack of a permanent courthouse. A station of that size was made for the overnight stay of a person too drunk to get home, giving misbehaving teenagers a good talking to, and not much else. Most of the job of the police force in Milhaven was to provide peace of mind.

"Deputy, please take Simon into the other room, we'll call his dad to come get him."

"No!" Beverly cried out.

Simon was pulled away, and she was led into a separate room.

The door closed behind her.

1 3

T he room Beverly was placed in was cramped and impossibly cold, with stiff, grey walls and no windows. It was impossible to tell how much time had passed as she sat there. Beverly had gotten up from the chair she was meant to sit in, and began pacing back and forth, her mind replaying the events of the day. Being alone in silence can be infuriating, even maddening, but it wasn't silent in the room. Beverly wished it had been silent. She could hear murmurs through the walls but couldn't make out any of the words. She couldn't handle not knowing what was going to happen to Simon.

She could only assume that half the town knew about what had happened by now—that she and Simon had been taken to the police station, that Elijah was nowhere to be found. The small town of Milhaven was filled with gossips, people who needed to know every little detail about everyone. If the wrong person heard something or witnessed something through parted curtains, most of the town knew before nightfall. Of course, that's the way it was. Milhaven was an incredibly fragile town, and Beverly was just beginning to understand that.

The door opened. The sheriff walked in, and he carried in with him a cool breeze from the front door. The loud slam of the door shocked Beverly, and she straightened up instinctively. Although Beverly had been confronted by the sheriff at the mines, this experience was different. She faced him alone this time, without Simon, and just two chairs and a desk to separate them. A cold cup of coffee was placed on the desk.

"Hello, Beverly," the sheriff said. He seemed more composed than earlier. His urgency hadn't changed, just his demeanor, his anger was contained now. "Are you willing to answer some questions for us?"

He sat in one of the chairs and invited Beverly to do the same.

"Of … yeah, of course, sheriff."

She took a seat.

"Thank you. And, don't worry, you're not being arrested, we're just talking right now. So … what is your relationship to Elijah Evans?"

Elijah Evans. Of course. He's the officer's real priority. Beverly realized that the officer only cared about Elijah's safety: what happened to him, what to tell his parents, whether or not she killed him. Beverly wished she had killed him. Her mind kept racing back to the moment when she was with him in the mines. How easy it would have been to kill him. She wondered if her conscience could have handled it if she had.

"We're friends."

The sheriff looked at her in disbelief. The police station didn't have a lie detector, but if it did, Beverly would have been hooked up to one after that comment.

"You and the Evans boy? You're friends?"

"Yes." It was all Beverly could manage to say. It was impossible for this sheriff to believe that she and Elijah could ever be friends. It was the exact same thing that Beverly thought when she first met Elijah.

"And how did you get to the mining site?"

"Elijah drove me."

The sheriff continued to give her the same look of visible skepticism. "And you drove out of town boundaries with him of your own free will?"

"Yes."

"Were you fully aware at the time that the Milhaven mining site is off-limits to civilians?"

"I could have guessed," said Beverly.

He stopped and gave her a sharp look before continuing. "What did you and Elijah Evans go to the mines to do?"

"Nothing, sheriff. Just look around."

"So, what happened to Elijah Evans? Where is he now?"

"He ..." Beverly looked down at her hands. "He skipped town. Left me at the mine site, drove off, he's probably miles away by now."

"He *ran away?*" The sheriff looked at her in complete disbelief.

"Yes."

The formality in his voice dissipated into a rougher, more aggressive tone. He leaned forward, lowering himself to her as if he wanted to speak off the record. "And you just expect us to believe that?" He shook his head. There was a look of pure disgust on his face.

For a moment, there was silence.

"I don't think you understand how bad this looks for us," the sheriff said slowly. "Now, I am going to ask you one more time. What happened to Elijah Evans?"

"I already told you."

"That's your final answer?"

"Um, I don't think I'll be talking anymore without Daniel present."

The police officer huffed, getting up and leaving the room.

Beverly sat alone in silence until she could hear a familiar voice coming from outside the door. She stood up, moving around the table to eavesdrop.

"Why wasn't I called earlier?" Daniel's voice boomed from somewhere in the front reception area.

"She hasn't been here long."

"Is she being charged with anything?"

"Not as of now."

"Do you have any evidence? Witnesses? Probable cause?"

"Not as of yet."

"Then, will you detain her any further?"

There was silence. Beverly was shocked to hear Daniel speak with such authority. She had never heard that tone from him before.

Footsteps tapped just outside the door, and Beverly ran to sit back down in her seat. A man she had never seen before walked in, a stranger in a police uniform with a scowl on his face.

"No charges are being filed against you, Miss Tailor. You are free to go."

Beverly stood and left the room. She walked down the hallway and found herself in the front room, which was filled with five adults that she didn't know, all giving her rough looks.

Daniel met her in the front reception area. "Hey," he said. "I'll drive you home."

Beverly shoved open the door, walked outside, and slid into the truck without a word. Simon's car was still in the parking lot, but Simon was nowhere to be found. What had happened to him?

It's all my fault. It's all my fault. The words repeated in Beverly's head, louder each time. She kept her eyes trained on the street as Daniel drove home, refusing to look up at the sun-streaked scenery the old town had to offer. It was the worst feeling of loss to be back in Milhaven after promising herself she'd never, ever come back—after being promised that she'd never have to.

"Are you going to tell me what happened?" Daniel asked, halfway through the drive.

"I figured they told you."

"They told me you left town at the exact same time Elijah Evans went missing."

"I don't want to talk about it."

"Yeah, well, maybe I do." Daniel raised his voice. "I don't think you understand how bad this looks for the both of us! I told you to keep a low profile, we were gonna do everything we could to make a good impression …"

"Well, I'm sorry if this is bad for your image."

"You know that's not what I mean!" Daniel shouted.

"Well, what do you want, Daniel? I didn't kill him, if that's what you're wondering."

"Kill him? No! Beverly, even if you don't like it, we're in this together now. The two of us, in this goddamn town, and I mean, people talk. I'm working my ass off to set you up with a good life, trying to keep us under the radar, and you go ahead and do … I don't even know exactly what you were doing, or why you did it, but I'll have to answer for it. I'm just …"

"Stop," said Beverly. "You're not my dad, and my mistakes aren't yours to own up to. God, I shouldn't even be here—"

"And yet you are," Daniel said. "What are you going to do about this?"

The car pulled into the driveway. Beverly's face tightened, her fists balling up at her sides. She could feel anger boiling up her throat, so she jumped out of the truck and ran inside the house. It didn't even feel real. She was supposed to be in a car right now, escaping all of this with Elijah, halfway to Mara's home. This house was her past, and it felt wrong to be here now.

Beverly rushed upstairs as Daniel made his way into the house.

"Good!" Daniel yelled out to her from the doorstep. "Just run away, again!"

"You think I'm wrong to run away?" Beverly shouted back, louder. "Where the hell were you when Dad died?"

Daniel said nothing.

Beverly scrambled into her room and slammed the door behind her. Tears blurred her vision, her back slammed against the door, and she slid all the way down to the floor.

1 4

At 11:50 a.m., two days after Elijah had left her on the floor of a cave, Beverly woke up. She didn't bother to wonder what day or what time it was. She was alone in the house, and Daniel hadn't woken her up for school. Ever since they got to this town, Daniel had hounded Beverly about not missing school, because people in a small town like this were more likely to notice an absence. Beverly knew that Daniel must have chosen to let her stay home despite all that, because at this point, staying home was less damaging than going out.

It didn't feel like a new day at all. It felt like the previous night had just refused to end. She was lying in bed, the sheets and blankets a twisted mess around her legs, but she didn't fix them. She didn't have the will. Beverly hadn't had a shower for two days now. Her hair was greasy, and her arms and hands were still bloodstained and lightly scraped. But it was more than just the dirt she felt on her skin. She felt unclean inside. She kept looking at her wrists, feeling her shoulders, the places on her body Elijah had grabbed when they were in the cave. Was that even a memory she could trust?

Against her stronger instincts, Beverly rolled out of bed. She stumbled into the shower, trying to avoid seeing her own face in the mirror. After a long shower, she scrubbed her body off with a towel and threw on a simple T-shirt and jeans.

Beverly crept down the stairs, finding that most of the lights were off. The living room curtains were closed, and the only light was coming from the fixtures that hung above the bar, separating the kitchen from the living room.

Beverly found that Daniel was home after all, sitting alone under the hanging lights, a glass of whiskey clutched in one hand with the bottle close by. It didn't look like his first. His head rested in his other hand, his thumb and fingers pressing against his temples, eyes closed.

Hearing her footsteps, Daniel's head snapped up, his back straightening immediately. He twisted around, noticed Beverly, and sank back into his defeated slouch.

Despite the lack of a welcome, Beverly sat across from Daniel. He looked up from the counter just enough to make eye contact.

"Look," Beverly said plainly, "I made a mistake. I should never have gotten involved with Elijah. But, you should have never gotten involved with that family in the first place."

"I know," Daniel blurted out, sitting up fully now. "God, do you think I don't know that?"

Beverly tried to muster up a response, but couldn't think of one. Daniel might have been one reason she was stuck in this town, but it wasn't really his fault. In all his regret, this was the first time Beverly had ever really felt as though she were on the same side as Daniel.

"What did they say to you at work yesterday?" she asked.

"Nothing," said Daniel. "They said absolutely nothing about it. I don't know what this means for me. I needed this job to take care of you, but now...I can't get out of it now, I—"

"I'm sorry," was all Beverly could offer.

"No," said Daniel, through a heavy sigh. "It's not your fault. I should have told you what I was doing here. You were going to find out anyway. I shouldn't have brought you to this town in the first place, you didn't deserve any of this."

"It's gonna be okay," said Beverly.

"What were you doing with him, anyway? What happened?" asked Daniel.

It was a good question, one Beverly didn't know if she had a real answer for yet.

"He … he told me he'd run away with me, take me to Mara's. Then we stopped at the mines, and he left without me."

Daniel looked down at his lap. "You thought he was gonna take you home?"

There was so much pity in Daniel's voice. It made Beverly cringe.

"Yeah," Beverly said.

"I'm … I'm sorry you're not back with her right now."

Beverly just nodded. None of this was his fault.

"So, what can we do now?" Daniel asked desperately. He was at his wit's end and wasn't thinking clearly. Daniel clutched his drink hard enough for his knuckles to turn white. His hand was beginning to shake, either from the whiskey or the stress, or a combination of the two. He had never been so frank with Beverly. At that moment, he wasn't just her guardian and she wasn't just a kid he was stuck with. They were in this together, as unfortunate as that was.

"I'll lay low this time, I promise," Beverly said. "I can stick with my story that he ran away, and we'll ride it out for now."

"Okay," said Daniel. "Okay, we can do that. I'll lay low at work, and I'll start to separate myself from the company. In just a month or two, we'll be able to leave this town of our own accord. I think I can do it."

"Okay," Beverly exhaled.

"But, you've got to do one thing," he said. "You need to go to school."

"School?"

"You eventually have to go, sooner rather than later. I get taking some time to recover, but you can't hide at home forever. Innocent people aren't afraid of being seen. Can you do that?"

"But—"

"Can you do that?" Daniel asked, speaking slowly and sounding sincere.

"Yeah. Yeah, I think I can."

It was just weeks ago that Beverly made a promise to Mara that she had no intention of fulfilling. She had told Mara that she would give Daniel a chance, give Milhaven a chance, and she hadn't. She thought it was time to start following through on her promises.

The next morning, Beverly pawed through the pile of laundry on her floor looking for something to wear on her first day back at school. Something simple, something with neutral colours that would draw the least amount of attention. She declined Daniel's offer of a ride to school, afraid that being one of the eight or so cars in the parking lot would just shove her further into the spotlight.

As Beverly walked through the halls of Milhaven High wearing her most unassuming expression, the crowd of students parted, with almost every eye watching her. Unable to ignore it completely, she continued down the hall, letting her instincts lead her to her locker, as though it were any normal day. Even without the stares and whispers, walking the halls felt strangely foreign to her, almost surreal.

Beverly had been moved around a lot, especially when she was young. She often found herself wondering, unwittingly, if she was standing in a certain place for the last time. She constantly worried that she'd have to up and move for some reason, leave town, go to another city, never to go back to that place again. It was an odd phobia, a sort of obsession that wouldn't let her live in the moment. This situation was almost the exact opposite. She had never imagined that she would be anywhere near this school ever again.

Beverly finally reached her locker only to see, plastered on the door, what looked to be the front page of the school newsletter: 'Elijah Evans Missing—Further Investigation Yet to Be Announced.'

Beverly tore down the page without reading it, desperate to minimize the number of people who would see it. She felt surrounded, panic-stricken by the people watching her with fear in their eyes, as if they were watching a wild animal from a distance. Beverly crumpled the newsletter in her fist, storming back down the hallway, avoiding eye contact. That walk almost became a run as her breathing grew heavier and she got dizzy dodging onlookers. A cold hand gripped her arm when she had almost made it outdoors. She turned to find that it was Simon holding her in place.

She knew the hand around her arm was meant to calm her down, but it only worsened her panic.

"Bev," said Simon, his face awash with concern, "let's skip first period today, okay?"

"Okay," she exhaled.

Beverly didn't know where Simon was leading her. He walked her around the building and behind the school. It was an area that gradually transitioned into the forest: all pavement and old fences and power lines, with a grouping of trees not far away. Beverly got nervous, wondering if people were going to see them together, skipping class.

"What happened to you?" Beverly asked.

"Nothing."

"Really?" she pressed. "Nothing?"

"Well, they asked me some questions," Simon said. "But they had no reason to keep me. Our story checks out, and they don't like that. What about you?"

"The same thing, really. Daniel was shocked they just let me go …"

"I'm not surprised. It's not just the police you have to worry about, though. There are a lot of people who can't believe Elijah would run away from his parents, and would love to have a scapegoat for his disappearance."

"But nobody thinks I actually killed him, do they?

"There may be some people who want you to take the fall for him. People who would rather believe Elijah is dead, than he deliberately ran away from his parents. The Evans family has a reputation to keep, and this doesn't bode well for them."

"So, this is all about the Evans family's image?" Beverly asked.

"Well, it's kind of more than that. What Elijah probably didn't tell you is that when he left, he took a hell of a lot of money with him— not his parents' money, but money from his parents' clients. That money was really important, and Christopher's parents say that everyone who works for them is in crisis mode right now."

"Because of me."

"Well, they …" Simon looked as though it hurt him to say it. "Some people might be thinking that you killed Elijah to get the money."

Beverly took a sharp breath in, her eyes becoming glassy as she held back tears.

"I'm so sorry …" Simon said, his eyes filled with worry, his face tense.

Beverly could remember so vividly what Simon looked like the very first time he saw her. How his whole face lit up when he said 'hello.' But now, under the shadow of the school, he looked so afraid, so sorry for her. The pity was something Beverly had seen often, but the fear in Simon's eyes was enough to bring her to tears. He didn't deserve any of this.

"Look, I … I never got the chance to apologize at the mine site."

"Apologize?" Simon's face fell. "For what?"

Beverly frowned, her gaze lowering to the ground. "When you asked me to Rosie's, I shouldn't have stood you up, you didn't deserve that … God, I can't believe I believed him, I shouldn't have gotten in his car, this is all my fault."

"It's not," Simon assured her. "Don't blame yourself for what Elijah did to you. None of that is on you. Bev, everything's going to be okay."

'Bev.' It was the name Elijah always called her, but it sounded different on another person's lips. Elijah always said it so flippantly. He decided on the nickname for her shortly after meeting her, not nearly enough time to get to know a person. It had shocked Beverly when he called her that, as if he claimed to already have some kind of a relationship with her. If only she had known back then, that it was all strategy and deception. But Beverly listened to Simon call her 'Bev' so gently, with no intentions behind it at all, just seeking to console. It was too kind. Beverly cried.

Simon reached around her, wrapping her in a hesitant embrace.

He wasn't sure why she was crying, but he was certain she had reasons, her last few days were full of them. Beverly's hand rested on top of Simon's shoulder, and she was afraid her tears would soak through his jacket.

A car pulled up behind the school and parked haphazardly near Beverly and Simon. Simon jumped a little, his eyes widening as he caught his breath. "Um, maybe we should make our way back?"

"Yeah, maybe we should." Beverly wiped her face with the sleeves of her sweater, a faint chuckle escaping her lips.

The pair slowly walked back to the front of the school, but there were other students who had the idea to cut class and get some fresh air, too. Beverly recognized some of their faces from the night of Christopher's party. A group of boys were gathered around the side of the school, and a few of them made direct and unapologetic eye contact with her. Beverly couldn't look away from them, causing her to lose focus on Simon's words, their stares almost physically knocking her off balance.

"Hey, Simon?"

"Yeah?"

"There was something else I needed to tell you," Beverly said.

"What's that?"

"Something I wanted to show you. Letters, a diary almost, left by the guy who used to live in that abandoned house. I found it at the poetry night thing ... it has all this stuff about the Evans family, people he thought they killed, exact dates and times."

"And, it's still there?"

"Yeah, it is. In his bedroom."

"Bev ... that sounds like evidence! Like, real evidence we could use against these people. We could bring it to the real police, in another town or something. We need to get it."

"Well, I was afraid to move it, it's still in the house. I'll show you where I hid the papers, we can go there now."

"No," Simon said firmly. "It's your first day back. I think you should go home, people might be watching you, just lay low and stay safe. How about tomorrow morning, we can meet there before school, and we'll bring it to the police in the nearest city."

Beverly felt stupid for not doing that herself in the first place, so none of this would have happened. She wasn't entirely on board with waiting until morning to go get the textbook she'd stashed the letters in, but she wasn't going to argue with Simon.

"Okay, I'll see you then."

Simon nodded and went back into the school as Beverly walked all the way home. She had done nearly everything wrong in her time at Milhaven, but she was determined to do this one thing right.

15

It was a chilly morning when Beverly Tailor began her walk to the abandoned house. Her pace was slow, disheartened. She knew she was facing a day of glares and stares between classes, backhanded comments from students, and silence from teachers. She reminded herself with every step forward that her morning would be spent with Simon, and she felt better. First, though, she needed to stop by the post office.

Beverly had not heard from Mara for nearly a week. She couldn't fathom an answer as to why Mara didn't respond to her letters. Even though Mara was responding to lies, to letters packed with false information, it gave Beverly comfort to know that she was at least alright. Beverly was getting restless. She knew that the post office in Milhaven was less than efficient, but she couldn't help but think there was some other reason she wasn't receiving Mara's correspondence.

She stopped outside the post office, taking a moment to stare at it with curiosity. If it were even possible, the place seemed to have gotten even sketchier-looking since the last time she was there. Its cement sidewalk seemed to have more cracks in it, and the 'Open' sign on the other side of the glass seemed to be hanging a little lower. Beverly pushed open the door, hearing the tiny brass bell ring above her. It was the same desktop counter facing her as last week, and the same thirty-year-old guy sitting behind it, reading the same dated sports magazine, an issue from at least five years ago.

"Hey, Tom?" Beverly asked, figuring she'd get a better response if she used the man's name, one she'd read off the tag pinned to his shirt on her last trip to the post office.

The man looked up from his magazine, although he must have heard the bell chime, he looked surprised. He wasn't happy to see her.

"What is it?" asked Tom.

"I'm looking for any mail for Beverly Tailor?"

"Sorry, kid, I got nothing."

"Are you sure? From a Mara?"

"I told ya, kid, I don't got nothing for ya. Sorry. I'm taking my break out back now. If you get any mail, I'll let ya know."

Tom took his magazine and disappeared behind a door to the back, leaving Beverly alone in the post office to show herself out. She almost opened her mouth to shout out her frustration, but stopped herself. She knew screaming wouldn't have helped. Instead, she stood there angry, waiting, staring at the door that had just slammed shut. Unsatisfied, Beverly's eyes wandered behind the counter, beginning to wonder if Tom did any work at all, or merely pretended to.

Beverly wasn't surprised to find that it was a total mess behind the counter. She saw stacks of magazines, food wrappers, letters and parcels lying in piles that feigned organization. As Beverly rose up on her toes to see more on the other side of the counter, she saw a large stack of envelopes held together with thick rubber bands. On the top envelope, she could almost make out her name. Beverly's heart raced, trying to think of a way to get the letters without letting Tom hear her. Just as she determined that she could, in fact, hop over the counter inaudibly, the door that led to the back popped open.

"What the hell are you still doing here?" demanded Tom.

Beverly pointed her finger at the stack of envelopes behind the desk.

"Those are my letters! You're withholding my mail!"

"Little lady, calm down, that's insane. You've got exactly zero proof of that. Now get out of here."

Now that she was being called out for it, Beverly did have to concede that the stack of letters was very far away, and that it was possible she'd read it wrong. She didn't like the fact that she was doubting herself, but there was no use in fighting with Tom. She felt her hands ball up into fists, her mouth forming a hard, straight line. She stormed out the door and back down the street. She kept walking down the road toward the school.

The scent of burning wood began to filter into the air, and Beverly quickened her pace. A cloud of smoke emerged over the horizon, filling the skyline just a few streets ahead of Beverly's destination, like a dark ghost wafting in the breeze.

A fire.

Beverly's grey sneakers slammed against the pavement as she ran, breathlessly, toward the smoke. She cut corners and crossed streets, rushing to get to the school, but she turned the final corner to find the school untouched by fire. The smoke was coming from somewhere else. She continued down the street, watching hordes of people gravitating toward the road's end, until Beverly saw what they were all crowded around. It was Stephen's house, engulfed in fire.

Orange flames consumed the building from the inside out. The glass from the windows had shattered, its shards strewn along the sidewalk. The crackling wood, which had proudly held the home together for decades, splintered, submitting to the fire. As Beverly moved closer, she could see the smoke seeping out of the house through the half-open door, the air outside fueling the fire with more oxygen. She could taste the thick, smothering sensation of air mixed with smoke moving down her throat. Every person on the street stood still, transfixed by the blaze. Why wasn't anyone doing anything?

It didn't take long at all for the police to arrive. The police car first on the scene held two of the town's three officers. After barrelling down the street, it came to a sharp halt, parking in the middle of the street. Both officers got out of the car, but neither attempted to get help, or stop the fire, or subdue the people watching. They didn't seem to make any effort to do anything at all. They were quiet, oddly solemn, just witnesses in the crowd of passersby.

As the flames filled the house, Beverly was so hypnotized by the scene that she barely noticed Simon and Christopher rush up behind her. She turned to find that Simon was wearing a look of urgency on his face.

Christopher spoke first. "Beverly, we need to get you out of here, right now." His hand was on her shoulder, ushering her away from the fire.

"What's going on?" Beverly demanded.

She never got an answer. They just ran, not daring to look back, as if the growing flames were chasing them. They passed strangers who were trying to make their way toward the fire, gawking at the burning house, wondering how far the flames would spread.

Christopher led them all the way to the door of his house. They piled in, and the door was slammed behind them.

"Beverly," Simon said through a choked breath, "I think someone must have overheard our conversation yesterday,"

"The fire wasn't an accident," said Christopher. "They thought you two were in that house this morning, it's the only explanation, they're targeting you two."

Beverly's heart dropped. The fire was meant for them—meant to swallow them whole. She felt unsteady all of a sudden, so she stepped back and sat down on a couch, her mind spinning. "They were targeting us? Who's 'they'?"

Simon took a seat across from her, with a troubled look on his face. "The Evans family, they were trying to destroy the evidence."

"They were one step ahead of us," said Beverly.

Beverly wished she were a million miles away. It felt as though the smoke was still reaching its way down her throat, just daring her to cry.

"What do we do?" Beverly asked in desperation. What an unfair question that was. She had just caused this whole terrible mess, and now she was asking Simon and Christopher what 'we' should do about it. There was no 'we' in this situation—just a problem, and two kids who'd gotten sucked in as collateral damage.

"We've got to fight back," said Simon. "They can't do this. The Evans family has had a hold on this town for too long. It's not safe anymore, and we've gotta do something."

Caroline burst in through the door.

"God, Carey!" Christopher threw himself into his girlfriend's arms.

When they separated, Christopher locked the door, turned down the lights, and closed all the blinds. Beverly didn't think that just locking the door would do much to defend against a group of people unafraid to burn the things that threatened them, but she didn't bother saying that. In fact, she didn't feel as though she could say anything. Her throat tightened, and she did everything she could to stop her hands from shaking.

Christopher, Simon, and Caroline all stood in a little circle attempting to strategize. Beverly thought they either looked like world leaders during wartime or little kids deciding on what game to play next, she couldn't decide which. They talked and talked about how evil the Evans family was and how this was the last straw. Beverly just sat there, staring down at her trembling knees with absolutely no plans on getting up. She zoned out.

Beverly wasn't meant to be there, not in Christopher's living room, not in Milhaven at all. She was meant to be with Mara, who now felt impossibly far away. Mara wasn't even a post office trip away anymore. Beverly wondered if she'd ever get to see Mara again, if she'd survive in town long enough to make her way back home. She couldn't think of any plan the scheming teenagers could dream up that would get her home with Mara any time soon.

Even if she did go home to Mara again, she wouldn't be the same as before. Milhaven had changed a part of her. She wasn't the same quiet foster kid; she didn't really feel like anyone's kid anymore—just a burden, a suspected killer on the loose. What would Mara think of her now, now that people saw her as a criminal?

Beverly heard her name come up in conversation and her watering eyes glanced over to Christopher.

"But, Beverly's uncle doesn't have anything to do with it."

"Daniel?" Beverly asked. "What about him, is he gonna be okay? I gotta go see him."

"He's gonna be fine," said Caroline. "Wherever he is, I'm sure he's okay, and it'd be safer for him if you don't see him right now."

Beverly wasn't satisfied with that answer. "But, what's going to happen to him?" she demanded.

"I don't think anything, they don't want anything from Daniel. We think you'd be safest here," said Christopher.

"For now, maybe," said Beverly. "But, if they suspect us already, won't they find us sooner or later?"

"We have a plan," said Simon.

Beverly looked up at him, and then to Caroline, who was flashing a bright smile behind him.

"We can't try to fight the Evans family or the people who work for them, it's just not possible," Caroline explained. "I know for a fact that the Evans workers have meetings at the town hall past curfew, they're meeting sometime in the next few days. I overheard it from my parents, they were talking on the phone about it. I think that tonight, we should go into the town hall and bug the place. If we hide microphones, we can record what they say, and then show it to the police. Like, the real police, in the nearest city. It's our best option."

"We can keep you here in this house until then," said Simon. "Nobody'll know you're here, Christopher's parents won't be home for another few days. You'll be safe until we can make it to the police."

"I can do that, I guess," Beverly said.

"So we hide in here, and then at night, Simon, Caroline, and I go out and bug the place, then we come back. In and out, quick as we can."

"I want to come," Beverly stated firmly.

"You should stay here," urged Caroline.

"No. I've gotta be there, too."

Christopher interjected. "But, it's too risky for you—"

"It's too risky for you to keep me in your house in the first place. I'm coming with you."

The three kids agreed that Beverly would accompany them, but there was still a lot of time before they could go out to the town hall. The house was still dark, with every door locked, every window latched shut, and every blind drawn. The four kids were effectively under house arrest, dormant until midnight.

Beverly went to the basement for the same reason the king sits at the back of a chessboard. It was clear to Beverly that the fire had been meant for her. The police made a promise to follow up with her, but she wasn't so much afraid of the police showing up at her door. She was afraid of the town, of the people who set the fire, of Mr. and Mrs. Evans. She had taken one of their own from them, or at least that's what they wanted to believe. This town didn't know anything about justice, only vengeance, a vengeance that could come for Beverly's loved ones as easily as it could come for her. Beverly texted Daniel to let him know she was safe, and staying the night at a friend's house.

After ten minutes of sitting alone, Simon came down the steps to join her.

"Hey," Simon said, taking a seat next to her but keeping a cautious distance. "Are you alright?"

"I'm sorry," blurted Beverly. "I'm really sorry, all of this, it's all my fault, I was so stupid, going with him, I—"

"It's fine."

"Is it fine?" she whispered. "Is it fine that, because of me, a house got burnt down, I mean, someone … you could have been in there."

"Nobody was though, Beverly, no one died—"

"Yet, Simon! Nobody's dead yet, but it could have happened so easily, and if I had been smarter, everything would be fine."

"You're being way too hard on yourself. There was no way you could've known this would happen. You shouldn't beat yourself up over it. It was Elijah's fault, no one else's. And he's gone now."

Images of Elijah came flooding back to her all at once. When she closed her eyes, she could see the look on his shadowy face when he'd left her alone in that cave.

Beverly had thought that her persisting fear of Elijah was irrational, until she remembered that there was nothing stopping him from coming back. Sure, Beverly thought to herself, he said he detested the town, but there was no way to know if anything he'd ever said to her was true. She imagined him coming back, finding her, hurting her, hurting her friends. She didn't like the fact that he knew where she was, but she didn't know where he was. She took no comfort in the idea of seeing him again. He was all that was on her mind since she left the cave. But she couldn't say any of that to the boy in front of her. If she had just listened to Simon, none of this would have happened.

Beverly buried her face in her hands, as she fought for a deep breath.

"You're right," Beverly exhaled. "He's gone."

Simon gave a sympathetic smile.

"Do you really think this plan is going to work?" asked Beverly.

"Yes. Or at least I think it's our best shot."

"But, it's so risky, especially hiding me here, you have no idea what could happen."

"I know what'll happen if we do nothing. I know that they'd find some way to frame you for Elijah's disappearance, and they'd take you wherever they put kids who kill people. Or worse."

"This isn't your responsibility, you know. Protecting me."

"I want to do it, though. I want this town to be safe enough for you to live in without being afraid."

Beverly shook her head. "You don't have to do this for me."

"I'm not," Simon said, his elbows pressing into his knees, his gaze unwavering. "I'm doing it for entirely selfish reasons. Because *I* want you to stay. Because *I* can't stand the idea of living in a town that takes in people like you and hurts them like this."

She looked at him with wide eyes and gave a smile that was faint, but warm. She had no idea what to say to him. Of course, it warmed her heart that he felt that way, but she wasn't as excited for what those feelings were driving him to do.

Christopher was with Caroline upstairs, pooling together all of their cell phones and other recording devices they'd need to become amateur spies, while Simon alternated between spending time with Beverly downstairs and cooking in the kitchen. His food was the best Beverly had eaten in Milhaven, but she didn't have the stomach for more than a few bites. She didn't want to show too much fear in front of Christopher, Caroline, or Simon. The last thing she wanted was for them to pity her even more than they already did. It broke Beverly's fast-beating heart that these kids cared about her well-being so relentlessly. Didn't they know that she'd caused this whole catastrophe?

There was a short time when all four of them were in the basement together, after dinner had been finished and all the recording equipment had been placed by the door; they were just kids, just for a moment, and the four of them put on a movie and watched it together. Watching a movie wasn't something any of them wanted to do exactly, they just didn't know what else to do.

Beverly sat beside Simon on the couch, watching as Christopher and Caroline talked over the movie, chatting about school and food and a million other things that seemed to matter so much less to Beverly now than they had a few days ago.

Normally, Beverly hated when people talked during movies, but something about Caroline's comments gave her the smallest amount of comfort, just enough to get her through the film. Silence was dangerous at a time like this, when the worst kind of thoughts were lurking in the shadows, on the edge of her consciousness.

The movie played and, as time passed, the tone in the basement got a little bit lighter. Simon, who had been sitting rigidly straight, began to slouch into the couch. At some of the best jokes, he would lurch forward, laughing with his whole body, and each time he would end up just a little closer to Beverly. Her eyes started tearing up again, but this time it was from laughter.

Christopher seemed uninterested in the movie that was playing, but he didn't complain about it. He was too busy watching Caroline, watching her eyes brighten when her favourite parts came on, watching her fingers absentmindedly drum against his skin during the boring parts.

After the movie ended, another one was chosen at random. At one point, all the food was gone, and the room grew quiet. Even Caroline had stopped talking. Somehow, the quiet didn't feel dangerous anymore. It felt incredibly safe. The voices on the screen droned on, but it felt as though there was nothing else that needed to be said.

A part of her, that she was not proud of, wondered if it was too late to run away. That maybe she could pretend to go get a glass of water or use the bathroom upstairs and find some way to crawl out a window and put as many miles between her and this wretched town as she could, and place herself in Mara's arms with the future she'd imagined for herself. Was that even possible anymore?

Beverly looked at the kids around her, the way Christopher held Caroline in his arms, and how Simon's hand inched toward hers. These weren't fighters or rebels. They were kids, just trying to help her and their families. This was what she would be leaving behind.

She did not run away that night, because home had begun to feel a little less far away.

16

As midnight drew near, it became increasingly obvious to the kids that they couldn't stay inside forever. Curfew had already passed, by almost an hour. Time had slipped away from them, and if they didn't leave, then they never would. As the credits of the last movie played, it was wordlessly agreed upon that the evening was over and the night had just begun.

Caroline argued that it would be less conspicuous to walk, but Christopher reminded her that the van would get them there and back quicker.

Spirits were still high at that point in the night, but there was still a solemn sort of air in the room as everyone pulled on their shoes and threw on their jackets. Yes, they were all still together, and yes, the evening had been just like any other evening with friends, but it was as though everything was going to change that night.

Second thoughts about their break-in bounced around Beverly's head. She didn't like this plan or the risks that came with it, but she understood that the stakes were high for her new friends, too. This was saving their hometown, a place they believed in. Beverly held no obligation to this town; it had never felt like her own. These people she met, they were trying to free their parents, do what they thought was right. Beverly respected that, even though the thought of Simon getting caught or getting hurt made her feel sick.

Christopher was the driver, and Caroline took the passenger seat. Simon and Beverly sat in the back.

When they arrived at their destination, Beverly quickly understood what the 'town hall' actually was. Caroline had told her the story of how the hall came to be.

Originally, it was the Holy Spirit Church, a Christian place of worship, built in the sixties. The place lost its purpose around the mid-eighties. Folks began going to church less and less often—those tied to the Evanses stopping first, the remainder of the congregation following in their footsteps. After only a few months of the church's congregation dwindling, Father Charles skipped town under mysterious circumstances. After his disappearance, the hallowed hall of the Holy Spirit Church was converted into a platform where the mayor and the Evanses could speak directly to the townspeople on important matters, like fall fairs and Christmas pageants and staying silent about the strange things that went on around town.

The building itself wasn't huge, but it stood tall. Its freshly painted white exterior was a stark contrast to the worn-down buildings it neighboured. A short set of stairs led to the church's entrance, a set of double doors with an empty flower pot on either side. The moonlight cast strange shadows down on the building. Christopher pulled into a parking space.

"No!" exclaimed Caroline.

"What is it?" asked Christopher.

"You've got to park *behind* the church."

"Why?"

"Well, what if someone sees our car in the front?"

"God, Carey, nobody's awake!"

"Still," insisted Caroline. Christopher put the car in reverse, drove it around to the back, and parked in a small area directly behind the church.

"Alright," said Christopher, looking toward the backseat. "This won't take long. We'll be in and out in five. See you soon."

Simon and Beverly nodded. Caroline offered Beverly a consoling smile, then made her way into the church with Christopher. They walked around to the front of the building in the darkness of night and went in through the main doors, which had been left unlocked. They looked around. Nobody knew where the meeting would take place, so they had to make their best guess.

"Carey, how about you go to the back rooms? There's not a whole lot of space, but it's possible they'll have their meeting there," Christopher whispered. There was no reason to whisper, but something about being in a nearly pitch-black church with such high ceilings cautioned him to temper his tone.

"Sure," she said. She walked tentatively down the aisle, disappearing into a back room.

Christopher was meticulous, but quick. He propped a cell phone carefully under a pew toward the front of the room.

After spending a few minutes in the dark room, his eyes had adjusted almost completely. He walked up the main aisle with confidence, toward the set of double doors, looking for a good place to hide the next phone.

Bright lights flashed through the window. They were coming from a steady stream of cars as they pulled into the church parking lot.

Christopher's heart nearly stopped. His body froze in panic, his knees buckled under him as he scrambled across the room. He ducked behind a pew, flattening himself against the floor. After a few painfully long seconds of silence, the door opened. Christopher prayed that it was somehow a mistake, a hallucination, until he heard a cacophony of voices and footsteps blundering inside all at once.

"And how the hell are we supposed to believe that he's actually dead?" demanded the first man. His booming voice travelled through the church, sending a shiver up Christopher's spine.

Christopher remained still, staring at his shoes, trying to control his own fragmented breathing.

"Look, Doug, it doesn't matter if we believe it, the Evans family does, and that's all that matters," replied a second voice. This one rang unmistakably familiar to Christopher. It was calmer, quieter, more assuring, but still managed to shake Christopher to his core.

"Dad?" he whispered under his breath.

THE MAN'S booming voice was loud enough for Caroline to hear all the way in the back of the church. She couldn't tell who it was, but she knew it was trouble. She crept into the closest room, looking frantically for somewhere to hide, her heart beating in her throat. Caroline realized that there was nowhere to hide in the dusty room. She rushed to the window, praying that it wasn't locked shut. Her hands were shaking, twisting the small white crank by the window. The window creaked as it inched open, and she could do nothing but hope that the walls were thick enough to stifle the sound.

After she closed her eyes for a moment, Caroline looked out the window and down at the grass. She hadn't realized how high the windows were from the ground. She found herself at least six feet from the ground.

Caroline tossed one leg over the windowsill, then the other. She turned her hands on the windowsill, gripped it tightly, and lowered herself as both her feet collided with the side of the building. After that, Caroline made a huge mistake—she looked down. Her body went rigid as she quickly realized the distance between her feet and the ground.

Voices and movements were still audible from the inside of the church.

She extended her arms in an attempt to lower herself farther. It was grassy below her, with some kind of unkept bush near the side of the church. It wasn't so much the impact, or even the promise of broken bones that she feared most, but the sound she would make upon impact— that's what she was afraid of—that she'd be noticed.

She loosened her grip and let go of the windowsill. She landed— the earth soft under her feet—tucked her body in, and rolled backward. Before checking for injuries, she tilted her head and found that

Christopher's van hadn't moved. Did Beverly and Simon even know what was happening? She ran toward them, disregarding her aching knees.

She scrambled into the driver's seat. Beverly and Simon just stared at her in shock.

"Carrie," said Simon, bewildered. "Did I just see you jump out of a win—"

"I just had to get out of there," Caroline cried, her voice pleading as she struggled to keep her breath.

"Whoa, hey, it's okay Carrie," Simon said gently. "Tell us what happened."

"There are people in there!" Caroline said through heaving breaths. "They came early, and Chris! He's still in there." She sank into her seat, her heart beating heavily in her chest, her head pressed against the steering wheel.

INSIDE THE BUILDING, Christopher remembered that because he never got to plant a device by the door, his phone was still in his pocket. He took it out and held it in his shaking hands. He opened up an old text conversation with Caroline and tapped out a message.

'I'm inside. Hiding. Safe. Where r u'

He hit send. A flood of relief came over him when a text came in immediately.

'I got out. With Simon and Bev. You'll get out soon. I love you.'

The male voices were booming and seemed to be moving around the room. Christopher flattened himself against the floor.

"Tailor?" A voice hissed. "Daniel Tailor? No, we can't trust him anymore. Not with his punk little daughter trying to compromise our operation. The Evans family are kidding themselves if they don't think she killed that little brat."

"Still, with the boy gone, we've lost all the assets he had. Plus the tens of thousands he took with him."

"How much you wanna bet the girl doesn't have that tucked away in her room somewhere? I bet Daniel and her planned this somehow. I can't believe that idiot of a cop just let her go ..."

"Don't worry, they won't let that continue much longer."

Christopher looked around. He was only about ten steps away from the door, but there was no way he could just get up and leave. He clutched his cell phone and typed out a message, trying desperately not to drop it.

'I love you too.'

He listed off his options in his head. He could stay there behind the pew for as long as it took for the men to leave. That was risky, because they could stay there all night. The longer he stayed, the higher the chances that someone would find him there. He could run, hoping to make it out the door before getting caught or recognized. He figured that would rely on the risky assumption none of the people inside were carrying guns. He stayed put.

IN THE CAR, Caroline peered around the corner, trying to see what was at the front of the church. She noticed multiple cars on the side of the street, at least six or seven.

"Simon, Chris taught you to drive, didn't he?" asked Caroline.

"Yeah, he did once. Why?"

"Because I need you to get in the driver's seat and bring us around to the front.

"What? Why would—"

Caroline turned around. Tears rolling down her cheeks disrupted the fierce look of determination that shaped her face.

"I'm going to need you to trust me."

She pulled out her phone and sent a message to Christopher.

'I'll distract them. When I do, run out and get in the car. Trust me.'

Caroline jumped out of the car. Simon shared a few seconds of eye contact with Beverly before he got out of the car and took a seat at the steering wheel. Caroline started running toward the church.

"Wait!" Simon cried.

Caroline grabbed a fist-sized rock from the curb. With laboured breaths and startling accuracy, she threw it directly through the church's stained-glass window. Shards of glass flew everywhere. She picked up another rock and sent it through the air, but this time it didn't hit her target, it hit the wall and ricocheted off. She did it again and again and again, her aim faltering as tears blurred her vision.

Inside the church, with the deafening sound of shattering glass, Christopher felt as though his heart had restarted. He bolted upright. The men watched the shattering windows in shock.

"What the—"

"Who's out there?"

"Is that Barry's little girl?"

Christopher used Caroline's distraction the way she had intended for him and scrambled out of the building. Just as he slipped out the door, he heard a resounding command from the inside of the church.

"Luke! Go, take care of her."

Christopher's sneakers pounded into the grass as he sprinted along the perimeter of the church. He collided with the van's door and threw himself into the backseat, climbing over Beverly.

"Drive," Caroline barked at Simon.

He hit the gas, tires kicking up mud and tearing up the lawn, but the van found traction and lurched forward, shooting out of the parking lot and down the road. It was no time at all until they made it to Christopher's house. Simon's rushed parking landed them partially on Christopher's front lawn. All four kids poured out of the car, dissolving into a huddle of hugs and sentences of three words or less.

"Oh my God."

"You're okay."

"I love you."

17

Caroline and Christopher had fallen into each other's arms on the front lawn, oblivious to the world around them. Christopher's trembling hands swept through Caroline's hair as she buried her face in his shoulder. As this happened, Beverly was the first to notice a dark grey van slowly twist around the curb and come to a halt. The moonlight reflected off the vehicle's glossy sheen. Beverly unravelled her arms from Simon's as she turned to say something to the others.

Beverly watched as the vehicle's door slid open. It was Luke.

The cold air had thickened, stiffening inside Beverly's throat, leaving her voice cracked and hoarse. "Chris!"

Christopher separated himself from Caroline as he turned to face the van at the side of his driveway.

Luke raised a gun in trembling fingers, his other hand gripping the top of the vehicle.

Beverly watched Luke close his eyes.

A blood-curdling shout escaped Christopher's lips. "*Wait!*"

A loud bang shattered the air.

The world fell silent.

Caroline clutched her stomach, her face blank. The van door closed, and the driver sped away. Christopher turned to Caroline as she began to stumble backward. He put one hand on her back and collapsed to the ground with her.

"No," whispered Christopher, as he propped her up against him. Caroline's stomach was oozing blood, soaking through her shirt. One of her hands was pressed to the wound, the other held Christopher's hand. He looked at her with wide, tearful eyes.

"Don't cry," Caroline managed. "Nothing's going to …"

"No, no, Caroline, you're going to survive this, please, just look at me, hey, look at me."

But she wasn't looking at him. She was looking past him.

"It's okay, Chris," she choked. "It's okay."

Beverly exhaled, her stomach wrenching with shock, grief, and sympathy. Simon stood beside her.

Christopher dropped his head, still clutching Caroline's hand to his chest. He laid her down, letting her head rest on the grass. Caroline's gaze drifted away from Christopher's face. She looked to the stars, as if to admire them for one last time. Her eyes glazed over.

"No," breathed Christopher. His hands were trembling, running through her hair, his throat swollen and raw. "No, no, no …"

Beverly and Simon looked at each other, down at their friends, and back at each other. They were paralyzed as Christopher crouched over Caroline's dead body.

Christopher was left whispering the word 'no,' over and over again into the night air, while painfully trying to recall the last words Caroline had said.

1 8

Four days after Caroline's body was carried into Christopher's house off the grass, a funeral invitation landed in Beverly's hands. It was given to her from her uncle, who had no idea how to comfort her at a time like this.

"Are you sure you're okay?" Daniel had asked her in a quiet voice, the night Beverly came home with tears in her eyes. Eventually, he stopped asking the question. Daniel didn't know Caroline or how much or how little the girl meant to his niece. He was able to make educated guesses, based only on Beverly's inability to leave her room for hours on end and her indifference to even the best of his home-cooked meals.

It seemed like Daniel was trying to be invisible. He floated around the house, hardly ever speaking to Beverly. He cooked meals every night and ate them by himself, while Beverly was in her room, and left the rest on the stove for Beverly to microwave for later.

Beverly opened the sealed envelope with meticulous care, making every effort to not damage the contents. She held the white card that she found inside and unfolded it. There was no picture of Caroline in the card, just words pressed in black ink, and a small illustration of a flower on the top of the page:

·

Celebrating the Life of Caroline Stoakes
We invite you to join us as we pay our respects
at the funeral of Caroline Stoakes.
November 20th, 4:00 p.m., 17 College Street

It was two days away. She hadn't seen or heard from Christopher since the night Caroline died. As far as Beverly and Simon knew, Christopher hadn't even left his house. Beverly was hoping that this funeral would be a chance to see him, to comfort him.

If she was being honest with herself, Beverly still had trouble believing that her friend was dead. She was sad and angry and afraid, but she was mostly in disbelief. She hadn't been to school; she was too scared to look Caroline's killer in the eyes—and not just the one boy who pulled the trigger—but the men who'd ordered him to do it as well, and the wealthy family who controlled those men. Beverly was too afraid to even go outside. She just peered out of her window and imagined the people walking past conspiring to kill her, too.

Beverly snapped out of her spiraling thoughts when she realized she was clutching the invitation in a fist. She dropped it, not bothering to pick it back up. She quickly turned on the local radio for a distraction and slumped back into the couch.

"—evening, the mayor will be speaking at the town hall, to address any questions or comments that citizens of the town might have on the—"

The phone rang in the stillness of the house and startled Beverly. She had altogether forgotten that the house had a landline. She didn't even know why the house was equipped with a phone, or why the Evans family would need its employees to have one in their houses. She picked up the phone hesitantly, holding it up to her ear and waiting.

"Bev," said Simon's voice on the other end. Beverly let out a breath. "Have you been listening to the radio?"

BEVERLY MET with Simon as per his instructions, about a block away from the town hall. Simon didn't want Beverly waiting around for him alone in the crowd. He didn't tell her that, of course. He only told her to meet him a block away and they'd walk to the town hall meeting together.

"How've you been doing?" asked Simon as he watched Beverly walking toward him. They began their slow pilgrimage to the town hall.

"I'm okay," said Beverly. She didn't feel justified in saying any more. She didn't know Caroline well enough, and although Beverly thought she was a beautiful, kind soul, with so many great qualities, she never had the connection with her that Simon and Christopher had. To Simon, Caroline was family. To Christopher, she was home. "And, how about you?"

"I'm just worried about Christopher," Simon said. It was a non-answer that Beverly expected. "Usually, I spend all hours of the day with him, but I haven't even seen him leave his house. He's replied to my texts, but only to say that he's alright."

"Well," said Beverly, "it's good that he could do that much."

Simon nodded slightly. "Yeah … I know. I just wish I could do more."

They had almost made their way to the town hall when Beverly noticed that she was getting a lot of strangers' attention.

"Are you sure it's safe for me to be here?" asked Beverly. She craned her neck as she scanned the side of the church. Where a stained glass window once stood, there was now only a hole in the building, boarded up with planks of wood and nails.

"Yeah, it'll be okay."

Beverly and Simon sneaked into the back of the hall. A couple of people who noticed her looked surprised to see that Beverly had chosen to come, sending a quiet barrage of judgmental looks her way. The Evans family, or what was left of it, sat in the very front of the room, showcasing their brave faces for the whole audience to see. Though neither Beverly nor Simon was able to see Christopher's face in the crowd, both of his parents were present, most likely ready to summarize the mayor's words for the radio, as well as whatever statements the Evans family might make. They never carried any recording equipment, only a pen or paper; their broadcast never featured quoted statements or recordings, only broad recaps of what had been said.

"Good evening, ladies and gentlemen," opened Mayor Flynn, after everybody had taken their seats and quieted down. "I'd like to thank all of you for coming today, especially on such short notice. I am here to speak to you all about the recent events in our town, to answer any questions you may have, and to allow the Evans family to give a statement. I'd like to invite Mr. and Mrs. Evans to come up and say a few words."

The town mayor gestured to the remaining members of the Evans family. The two parents moved toward the podium, though only Mr. Evans took the microphone. The mayor stood close by.

"Hello everyone," said Mr. Evans, his gaze steadying. His wife stood to the side, with her chin up and her hands folded politely in front of her. "I'd like to welcome you all to another town hall meeting. As you all know, my wife and I have been dealing with the disappearance of our son, Elijah, who went missing on Friday. We are still trying to understand the nature of his disappearance, and doing everything we can to get him back. We urge anyone with any information on his whereabouts or activity in the days before he went missing, to come forward, and help reunite us with our son. Thank you."

Beverly's hands were sweating and fidgeting, until Simon's hand rested over hers.

Mrs. Evans moved in front of her husband and the room fell silent.

A young girl stood up to speak, someone that Beverly vaguely recognized. "Could Elijah's disappearance be in any way related to the recent death of Caroline Stoakes?" This girl stood like the last tree in a burning forest, her voice clear and loud. Beverly remembered who she was as soon as she heard her speak. This was the girl who approached Caroline after they had gone to the coffee shop, who seemed so happy to see her. It was clear she was a good friend of

Caroline, but that was easy to guess, because everyone was Caroline's friend. She had been so loved.

Simon sat forward in his seat.

Mayor Flynn stepped forward. "The, um …" The mayor paused. "Thank you, miss, for your question. The investigation surrounding her death, as well as Elijah's disappearance, is still ongoing, so I will refrain from saying more at this time."

A murmur fell over the room, the mayor's comments sending discomfort and defiance throughout the audience.

"Are there any more questions?"

Several hands slowly raised into the air; these were all people who were concerned enough to speak but not defiant enough to speak out of turn.

"No questions?" The mayor ignored the raised hands. "Okay, well I think we can bring this town meeting to an end. Thank you, everybody," she said and left the podium.

As the mayor made her way to a back room, her anxiety evident in each shaking step, the whole crowd of people shot up, the same way people would jump after hearing someone shout 'fire' or after hearing gunshots. They were shocked. An uproar of noise came from the townspeople.

"Hey!"

"Where are you going?"

"She can't just leave—"

"What are you hiding?"

Beverly turned to look at Simon. "What do we do now?" Beverly asked, just loud enough to be heard over the roar of the crowd.

Simon scanned the room for Mr. and Mrs. Evans, then for their friends and for less friendly faces. "We should get out of here," Simon suggested, leading Beverly through the people and slipping out the back door. They rushed outside, ahead of the crowd. "Did you notice that?" Simon asked, not stopping.

Beverly had to almost run to catch up with him. "Notice what?"

"How the mayor checked her phone while Mr. Evans was speaking. Something surprised her, I think. Whatever it was, it must have been the reason she ended the meeting and ran off so abruptly."

Simon finally began to slow down, listening to Beverly but focused on the church entrance. Beverly studied him and could tell that he was watching the people who were beginning to file out of the town hall, trying to gauge their reactions.

Simon grasped Beverly's shoulder with a firm hand and pulled her sharply behind the building adjacent to the town hall and out of sight. Beverly let out an indignant sound but Simon had put a finger to his lips, indicating silence. They both watched as Mayor Flint jumped into her car and sped off, with the sound of tires squealing against pavement.

"Did you see which way the mayor went?" asked Simon.

"Toward the school, I think." Beverly didn't take her eyes off the road. "Let's follow her."

"Um ... how about I walk you home?" he offered, looking over his shoulder at the stream of people still pouring out of the town hall. "It's probably better for you to be out of sight after all those people come out here."

Beverly examined Simon's face. He looked concerned, almost out of breath. His head repeatedly swiveled around, his paranoia causing him to check his surroundings constantly. It was difficult for Beverly to see Simon so genuinely afraid. He was normally so comforting, so strong. Beverly looked to Simon as a figure of strength, but she knew that the town was starting to wear on him as well; she was determined to protect him, the same way that he had protected her.

It was a sunny afternoon, the day of Caroline's funeral. Time passed slowly under the hot autumn sun. Peering out her window, Beverly saw that the breeze outside had a certain way of making the leaves dance across her lawn. Today she wore a black, collared dress that she had only worn once, for the funeral of a cousin she barely knew.

Beverly realized her mind was racing dangerously fast. The service wasn't for another hour, but she couldn't stop pacing her room, her mind full of questions. As selfish as it felt, Beverly was worried about her safety. She was terrified that she was going to be confronted at the funeral. After all, she was a prime suspect for Elijah's disappearance; it was a wonder the police let her go in the first place. Even so, she couldn't miss Caroline's funeral. It just couldn't happen.

Beverly rooted through her closet to search for her black lace-up shoes for the funeral. They were nowhere to be found.

"Daniel!" she called out.

There was no response, which was unusual; when Daniel was home, he always answered when she called for him. The house sounded entirely too quiet.

"Daniel?" she called out again, quieter than she had meant to.

Beverly frowned. She was certain that he was home. Glancing out the window, she confirmed that Daniel's black pickup truck was still in the driveway. She also saw a small, white car haphazardly parked in front of the house, across the lawn.

Footsteps sounded behind her. She opened her mouth to shout, but something soft was pressed hard against her mouth, and no sound came out. Thick arms pulled her backward as she clawed at the hand over her face.

Everything went black.

HER HEARING RETURNED before her vision did. Consciousness came back slowly, first in the subtle murmurs of distant voices, then in the feeling of something hard and solid beneath her and something coarse binding her wrists. Beverly raised her chin slowly from her chest and pried her heavy eyelids open.

She was sitting on a grey fold-up chair in the centre of a huge, empty room. She was still wearing the black collared dress that she had chosen for her friend's funeral. She never did find her shoes, so the floor was icy cold under her socked feet. Her hands were bound with ropes, tied up in thick knots to the metal frame of her chair, twisting her arms at odd angles behind her back.

The room didn't look much like a room at all. It was too grey, too empty. It felt more like being inside a locked box. She wanted to scream, to call out, to cry, but her throat felt too tight to let out more than a whisper. Other people's voices murmured in the distance, beyond the door of the grey room. Fifteen feet in front of Beverly was a door. She couldn't see much from the small window at the top of the door, just another grey wall.

The voices and footsteps in the distance grew louder. Beverly desperately tried to pick out fragments of their conversations, before one voice rose above all the others.

"Boss! Boss, they say she's awake."

Beverly couldn't slow her heart pounding inside her chest or stop her hands from balling into tight fists. The heavy, grey door squealed open, and two people entered the room. In came Mrs. Evans, dressed in the same manner as the first time Beverly had met her. Her heels echoed across the steely floor in a way that made Beverly's skin crawl. Standing behind Mrs. Evans was Luke—Caroline's murderer. Standing close to Mrs. Evans, his lithe frame looked smaller than normal. Luke looked like some unassuming kid, despite the fact that Beverly watched him fire a bullet into one of the kindest souls she had ever known. Anger tightened Beverly's jaw.

"Miss Tailor, so nice to see you again," said Mrs. Evans. She looked like she was expecting a reply, but Beverly was struggling to look Mrs. Evans in the eye, let alone speak to her. She couldn't control her unsteady breathing.

Beverly's eyes wandered, unintentionally, from Mrs. Evans to Luke, who had his hands folded in front of him. He was playing the part of the bodyguard and watchdog. His eyes flicked up to meet hers for a split second before his gaze was fixed back down on the floor in submissive compliance. Beverly saw that Luke was probably just as afraid as she was. She wondered if, although she was the one tied to a chair, he might be just as trapped.

"So," Mrs. Evans began. She unbuttoned her blazer, a gun, barely visible, poking out of the lining of her jacket. She pulled up a chair and sat across from Beverly. "I just want to talk. Is that alright with you?"

They sat in silence, Mrs. Evans staring into Beverly's eyes, challenging her to speak. But Beverly didn't say a word.

"Perfect," Mrs. Evans said. "I'll cut to the chase. Something was taken from us, not too long ago—a very sizable amount of money. That money and the profits we get from investments are how we keep this town alive. We know that you stole it from Elijah, from us. We recommend you give it back to us, and you might just leave our little town unscathed. Your choice."

Beverly blinked, her trembling hands rubbing against the coarse rope. "I don't know what you're talking about, I haven't stolen—"

"We know you're lying." Mrs. Evans cut in, her tone icy and

patronizing, the high heel of her shoe tapping lightly on the hard floor.

Beverly swallowed, keeping her head up but her eyes down. She shifted in her seat and her eyes began to water. She didn't speak. Nothing she could say would change Mrs. Evans's mind.

"Now, if I were you," Mrs. Evans began, "I would be very, very careful with what you say next. I'm being polite now, but I'm sure you know how easy it would be to frame you for my son's death."

Beverly's throat went dry as she looked up at Mrs. Evans. She had never believed it was possible to hate a person more than she had hated Elijah. Beverly swallowed and used every spare ounce of nerve in her body to say something. "So, you know he's alive?" Beverly growled. "You knew I was telling the truth?

Mrs. Evans narrowed her eyes.

"I don't think you killed him. But, I know how much he wanted to leave Milhaven. I think you took advantage of him." Mrs. Evans took a breath. "I don't think you understand how good an offer you just received, Beverly. You come to my town, manipulate my son, steal from us, threaten our very livelihood. You'd be lucky to get out of this town alive ... or did you forget," Mrs. Evans taunted, "that your uncle works for the same family you stole from. Don't you think that might reflect poorly on him?"

The door flew open and Daniel emerged with a tall, thick-necked man behind him, pressing Daniel's neck with the end of a gun. Daniel winced at the cool metal against his skin, his chin pointed upwards, and his hands raised open palmed in surrender.

Beverly took in a sharp breath, searching for enough air to tell her how wrong she was. "It's not true," breathed Beverly. "Really, I didn't steal anything, neither did Daniel."

"Daniel has proved to be a valuable member of our team, but I would have never hired him if I'd known his daughter would cause me such a mess."

Beverly was speechless. She looked at her uncle in a new light; she had wanted to escape so she wouldn't have to be a burden on Daniel's life any longer, but now she realized how much her actions had truly affected him. His life was in a stranger's hands, and it was her fault.

"Bev, it's—" Daniel tried to say something, but the man dug the gun's tip harder into his skin, causing Daniel's shoulders to rise, his throat to choke up. The gunman's message was clear—this would be his only warning.

Voices in the distance got louder until the door opened and a man came inside, whispering something into Luke's ear. Luke's eyes widened and he turned to look at Mrs. Evans, who was still staring at Beverly with dead eyes.

Beverly took a moment to ground herself, her eyes trained on the floor below her. She tried to breathe as her vision blurred with every passing second. She raised her head, only to find Mrs. Evans facing her. Luke, who must have left the room at some point, crept back in without drawing attention to himself. He whispered something to the man holding the gun to Daniel's neck.

"Boss," said Luke.

"What is it, Luke?" answered Mrs. Evans, disinterested.

"It's just, boss, there are people surrounding the estate. They want you and your husband to come out. It looks like they're gonna break in. Some of them have knives, rocks, I think a few of them might have guns, they're … there's a lot of them."

"You've got to be kidding me … *goddamn it.*"

The gunman's shoulders rose, his stress becoming visible both on his face and on Daniel's. Beverly feared for her uncle's life.

"You," said Mrs. Evans. "What do you know about this?" Her slender finger pointed at Beverly's face.

"Nothing," Beverly said. She was done lying.

"You're lying to me. I don't know what you think you're doing in my town, but if you want to make it out of here alive, you're going to tell me what you know."

Beverly struggled to suck in a breath. "I don't know anything."

Mrs. Evans's mouth hardened into a straight line and her jaw set. She looked over at the man standing by Daniel. "I'm going to go deal with that … then I'll deal with her."

Mrs. Evans ordered Luke to stay there and keep watch over Beverly and Daniel until someone returned. She told the man who was pressing a gun to Daniel's neck to follow her, and they left the room. Daniel gave a sigh of relief, but they weren't safe yet. His hands fell into a low surrender, his eyes still filled with fear. Beverly's gaze clung to the worn metal floor, her consciousness wavering. Luke closed the heavy door behind Mrs. Evans gently, to not make too much of a sound.

The sound of Luke's hiking boots against the floor reverberated in Beverly's ears. Her head snapped up when the boy produced a knife out of his pocket. He came forward, put a hand on the side of Beverly's chair, and gripped the knife.

"Don't touch me!" Beverly snarled at him.

"Shh!" Luke hissed back at her. The blade tore through the rope, freeing Beverly's sore wrists. Beverly winced in pain as blood rushed back into her fingertips.

"I don't know what you're doing, but—"

"Oh, shut up, Tailor. I'm letting you go. We were all told to reinforce the Evans Estate at all costs, so this building is going to be empty in minutes. I'll say your uncle overtook me, grabbed my gun, and I had no other option than to let you go. If anyone ever finds out the truth about this, they'll kill me, and you better believe I'll find a way to kill you first."

Beverly met his eyes for a few moments, then glanced back at Daniel who was as still as a post. She was confused by Luke's actions, but curious about his intentions. In that moment, she wanted nothing more than to ask him why he killed Caroline, if he was even sorry.

As though he couldn't handle her stare any longer, Luke stood up, turned around, and placed his own gun on the table. He put it down too hard, though, because his hands were shaking. Beverly watched him closely. This was the boy who had murdered Caroline in cold blood. Yet, as he stood facing Beverly, he was filled with so much fear.

"Did you hear me? I said go."

Luke blinked, turned around, and left the room, closing the heavy door behind him. Daniel ran to his niece. "Bev, oh, my gosh, are you okay?"

That was all it took for her to start crying. "Daniel, I am so, so sorry. This is all my fault, I never should have gone with him."

"Beverly, it's fine, it's okay, we just need to get you out of here."

Daniel picked up the gun from the table. Beverly wondered if he even knew how to shoot it.

He spoke again. "Look, I know that this must feel like a lot right now, it would have been better if I had never brought you here in the first place, but I just need you to leave with me, we'll get you to safety, I'll explain everything later. Okay?"

He stretched an open hand to her. She took it.

Beverly didn't know whether or not she liked the fact that her uncle knew his way around the building. It meant that, for the past few weeks, he'd been working for these people, for this cause. But, in this moment, it was the only thing keeping her alive.

They twisted through hallways, Daniel leading the way, with Luke's gun at the ready in front of him. Luke had been right; almost everyone in the building was gone, the place was practically deserted. The few people who still remained were busy, huddled in corners, disregarding all else in preparation of what seemed like war.

The rest of the building was very similar to the room that Beverly woke up in. The floors and the walls were the same: hard, cold, and metallic. The hallways were long stretches of exits, entrances, locked doors, and break rooms—not a window in sight.

After running down a very long hallway, Daniel stopped and opened a door for Beverly, a door that led not to a room, but to two sets of stairs: one going up and one going down. Daniel scurried up the set of stairs leading upwards and away from the room Beverly woke up in. Beverly followed Daniel upstairs, through a few more doors, and in no time at all, they broke open the poorly-lit building's heavy steel door and watery daylight shone in. Despite the fact that Beverly and her uncle had gone up several flights of stairs to get there, they were only at ground level. After the blinding light, the second thing Beverly saw was green: grass, bushes, and thick trees.

"Where are we?" asked Beverly.

Daniel had the gun stretched out in front of him again. Even though they were outside, they weren't out of trouble.

"We're about a quarter-mile from town, behind the Evans Estate."

Beverly and her uncle shuffled their way through the thick brush, tripping over the roots of young trees and pushing aside branches. This small forest was like any other, except for one key trait: it didn't sound alive. No birds chirping, no gurgling of running streams, just a quiet breeze whispering through pine needles.

"Normally, no one comes through this little track of forest," said Daniel. "There's a pathway underground, it runs from under the Evans house to the headquarters, where we just were. That's most likely how Mrs. Evans and the mayor are getting to the Evans Estate, to try and deal with what's going on there."

"But what is going on there?" asked Beverly.

Through the last strand of trees, Beverly and her uncle saw the back of the Evans Estate. A distant roar of shouting seemed to be coming from the other side of the house. It sounded like what Beverly assumed a riot would sound like.

"The people, they're fighting back. After Caroline's death, a lot of people had questions for the Evans family, and they didn't get any answers. Then the Morgado family, the family with the radio station, who work for the Evans's, I think they've gone rogue. Their boy called the whole town over to the Evans Estate over the radio, I have no idea where they are now."

"So, what are we going to do?" asked Beverly.

"I ..." Daniel trailed off, thinking of a good answer for her. "We're gonna leave this town now, and never turn back. We'll get out in plain sight, travel through the crowd. No one will notice we're gone."

Beverly couldn't bring herself to disagree, so they both quietly followed the perimeter of the building, as the voice of the crowd grew louder, more immediate. When Beverly and Daniel turned the final corner, they saw hundreds of people, so many that the crowd led all the way up the hill to the Evans house. The crowd was angry—no longer just neighbours—they were a mob, angry and dangerous.

BEVERLY HAD GONE to many concerts while she lived with Mara. For most of them, she went alone. She hardly even cared who was playing at the venue. She cared more for the experience, the people, the atmosphere. Beverly loved watching crowds of people by the hundreds, all cheering, belting out every word they knew, a whole world of lights and sounds and spilled drinks.

The sight that Beverly encountered at the Evans Estate was reminiscent of those concerts, but only in size and volume. There was a chorus of townspeople, all yelling angrily. They called out, demanding Mr. and Mrs. Evans come out the front door. A red brick soared through the air, shattering a tall window, sending glass spraying toward the crowd's feet.

Beverly and Daniel pushed forward, right into the heart of the crowd. Although the people were pushing back on them like ocean tides, this was the safest place for them to be. They weren't vulnerable to being targeted or singled out; they were a small part of a moving, faceless crowd.

Out of the corner of her eye, Beverly spotted a familiar face. Simon had found himself at the front of the mob, staring up at the house that lorded over him. Beverly was shocked to see Simon walk around to the side of the house, hop through a broken window, and dart inside the Evans Estate.

"Daniel!" Beverly cried from the very bottom of her throat. She turned to her uncle. "Someone … my friend, he just went inside."

"Inside? In the house?" he asked.

"Yes, why would he go in there?"

"Don't know, probably to find one of the Evanses, or to open the front door from the inside. Look, we have to leave, we've got to slowly make our way to the back of the crowd and get back to town, my truck is still in the driveway of the house, I still have my keys, we can make it out of here."

Beverly heard Daniel's words of hope, but her eyes wandered to the front of the crowd. A group of adults in work clothes were pouring something from red jugs at the foundations of the house and dousing the walls, the windows, the doors.

It was gasoline, Beverly realized, and Simon was still inside the house.

A man who was standing at the bottom of the staircase held a lighter above his head and threw it. Beverly's whole body lurched forward as she mouthed the word 'no,' her actions futile and hopeless. The lighter flew in the air, a tiny flame whizzing through the darkness of the night. Fire erupted, spreading itself up over the base of the building, blackening and burning the tall, white wooden staircase. The gasoline encouraged the fire to spread faster, farther.

Beverly broke into a run. Daniel pitched forward to grab her wrist, but he couldn't reach her. He wanted to call out her name, pull her back, tell her that now may be their only chance to escape. Instead, Beverly fought through the crowd, making her way to the very front, near the foundation of the house. She was surrounded at the forefront of the protest. The people to her left and right were the ones who had poured gasoline on the house, the ones who were crying out the loudest, demanding the powers that be to come out and take responsibility for their actions.

Beverly sneaked around the corner of the house, ducking in through the same low, wide-open window that Simon had jumped through. She threw one leg over the windowsill, then the other. She realized that she had been in this room before. It was the living room where she'd first met Mr. Evans. The room where she'd first met Elijah. A cloud of thick smoke drifted in through the doors and open windows. Beverly saw no flames inside yet, save the flickers of reds and oranges entering from the shattered windows, but the fire asserted its presence in other ways. Stifling smoke was paired with overwhelming heat. Beverly screamed out Simon's name over and over again.

There were two possible reasons, in Beverly's mind, why Simon had gone into the Evans's house. Either he meant to find the Evans family himself, or he meant to open the front door from the inside, to allow the protesters to come in and do it for themselves. Beverly realized that, because Simon had probably never been inside this maze of a house, he could be almost anywhere.

The smoke thickened in the air, billowing up the high ceilings. Beverly heard a stifled voice coming from deep in the house. It was loud, but she couldn't make the words out.

Beverly ran, blindly following the voice she thought she heard. She lifted the collar of her dress up over her face with one hand, hoping it would somehow filter out the smoke. Her socks tracked dirt and mud onto the clean carpets. Beverly navigated through the labyrinth of rooms, doing her best to remember the way from Elijah's tour. She realized at some point, while sprinting with squinted, strained eyes, that the voice could have come from someone else, other than Simon. It could have been anyone, even Mr. Evans, who might still be in the house.

Beverly had once been told, during a fire safety lesson in middle school, that you should shut all the doors in a burning building, because it deprives the fire of oxygen, stopping it from spreading. But she decided not to do this. Beverly had no interest in stopping this fire or even slowing it down. This building could burn. Beverly's only interest was in finding Simon, the boy whose name she was calling out over and over and over, through the stretched fabric of her dress.

She turned one final time, stopping in her tracks in a narrow hallway, her socked feet sliding on dirt and the hardwood floor. She saw Simon standing in front of her, with watery eyes and a hand clutching his chest.

"Beverly? Bev, is that really you?"

"Simon? Oh my God, Simon, are you okay?"

"You need ... I ... we have to get you outta here," Simon spluttered. "Bev, it's not—" His words dissolved into a fit of rough coughing.

Simon's wide eyes closed all of a sudden, and he fell forward into Beverly's arms, his body going limp. She took on his weight all at once and wrapped her arms around him. A flood of relief washed over her, but now she had to get them both out. She managed to hook her elbows under his armpits from behind so she could half-drag, half-carry him. The only problem with that was it meant she couldn't hold her shirt over her face, she was becoming short of breath, her breathing more shallow and strained. She dragged his body through the hallway while choking on the smoke. Just as her vision began to fail her, she pulled Simon's body up, with one unsteady arm gripping him around the waist. With her other hand, she clutched the searing hot doorknob and pushed open the heavy black door at the entrance to the Evans Estate. The door swung open, and she caught distorted glimpses of a massive crowd, flames raging in her peripheral vision. Just as the last remnants of strength fled her body, she stumbled forward.

The world faded to black.

BEVERLY HADN'T REALIZED how much time had passed when her bloodshot eyes opened and feeling came back to her body all at once. Something hard and solid was under her, and she realized she was lying flat on her back. Light streamed down over her face, cold and blinding, from round lights attached to a grey ceiling. She realized she wasn't in a room in two waves: first, she registered that the ceiling was only a couple feet above her face, and second, she noticed that she was moving.

"Beverly! Beverly, Doc, she's awake!" Daniel shouted over his shoulder, his voice raw. Beverly coughed, her body wrenching as she did, her eyes closed. "Daniel, where are ... did—" she spluttered through coughs. "Did we make it out?"

Daniel smiled, sliding over in his seat to hold her hand. "Yes, Beverly. We made it out, we're okay now."

Beverly allowed a smile to grace her face. Her eyes blinked open just enough to see Daniel's face looking back at her. She closed her eyes again, bursting into a fit of coughing that made lying flat on her back horribly difficult. Her cough sent her reeling up and forward until she rolled onto her side. Her eyes opened just long enough to see Simon laying on a stretcher next to her, with an oxygen mask over his face, his eyes closed.

The cool light that beamed onto Beverly's face from above turned hot. She closed her eyes—feeling as though she were falling forward, hard onto her feet—her head pounding.

She was back at the Evans Estate, in the wide-open living room. She wasn't in pain any longer. Instead, she was inexplicably numb. There seemed to be more windows in the room than Beverly remembered; they were all over the walls, black smoke flowing in from every window. The smoke enveloped her, wrapping her in a thick cloud that burned her eyes and crept down her throat. She ran away. Moving seemed easier for her than before; she could cut through halls and past rooms with no resistance, but the smoke still followed her. As she sprinted through rooms, out of the corners of her eyes, she saw fire light up, the flames climbing higher and higher the further away she got from them.

A sense of urgency overcame Beverly. She didn't know where she was going, but she knew that if she didn't get there in time, bad things would happen, everything would be ruined. It felt like the array of rooms was never-ending. New hallways seemed to appear one after another, a maze meant to trap her there forever. Nevertheless, she persisted, until at one turn she stopped in her tracks.

Elijah Evans stood in the corner of a room, in the same clothes he'd worn for their first meeting, just watching her.

"Why stop now, Bev?" taunted Elijah. "You can't slow down now. Time is not your friend."

Beverly screamed in horror before turning, running through the rooms, desperate to get away from him. Though Elijah stayed in place, his voice followed after her, telling her to 'hurry, hurry, hurry.' She ran, picking up speed, refusing to turn and look back at Elijah, in fear that he might be after her. As she sprinted through the hallways, fire crawled up the walls. The flames crackled above her, and the fire grew until it formed a circle around her, enveloping the entire room. The blackened curtains hit the floor, and suddenly, all Beverly could see were golden tongues of fire.

She could have sworn that amidst the flames, she could see the face of a woman. A woman that she hardly recognized anymore—her mother.

Beverly woke up again, flat on her back and gasping for air on the stretcher. As her body convulsed, a pair of hands pressed her back down. She quickly saw that it was Daniel who was pressing down on her shoulders in the hope that it might calm her down.

"Hey," he said. "You're awake again, thank God, you're awake. I'm going to need you to take some deep breaths for me. Yeah, deep breaths …" Daniel sounded like he was trying to convince himself that his own advice was sound.

He was a little frantic and was in no shape to drive the van, so the doctor, or the closest thing the town had to a real doctor, was behind the wheel of his own makeshift ambulance. The road to the nearest hospital was a long one, and it was left to Daniel to notify the doctor if something went wrong, to keep both Beverly and Simon alive until they got there. He shouted instructions to Daniel, occasionally stopping on the empty road to go back and help them when necessary.

"We're … we're out of the town now, aren't we, Daniel?" Beverly asked.

"Yes. Yes, Beverly, we've made it out. We're a lot safer now, we'll get you to a hospital soon, then home. Just, stay with me … you'll be okay."

"How is he?"

"Your friend? Oh, he was awake just a moment ago. He's breathing on his own now."

Something warm brushed against Beverly's hand. It was Simon, who wordlessly laced his fingers with hers. The touch sent waves of relief through Beverly, giving her enough peace of mind to allow her eyes to flutter shut. The van sped along the twisting and uneven road, rolling over rocky bumps toward an uncertain future.

Even as the spinning hands of time pushed forward, time seemed to pass ever so slowly as his hand held hers. She didn't know how home could feel so close out in the middle of nowhere, as if she could just reach out and touch it.

SIXTEEN MONTHS LATER

t first, it was the grandeur of the Evans Estate that Beverly found unnerving. She couldn't help but stare up at it in awe. It was even more staggering to see it in ruins.

Beverly stood dumbfounded, looking at the building's remains sitting atop the hill, untouched, sixteen months after a town set it on fire. Christopher stood behind her on a patch of dead grass, knowing enough to give her some space.

Left in the place where a house once towered, was now only its bare, burnt foundations. Beverly found her feet sinking into the rubble, as she wondered what the burnt objects on the ground were before they'd been ravaged by flames. She could make out a few chunks of windowsill, ceiling, furniture, a chandelier divided into six even pieces of tarnished silver. Some of the humble trees planted around the house had remained unscathed; the ones Beverly had once used as cover while sneaking out to Christopher's party, now towered over the remains of the house.

"God …" said Beverly. "You weren't kidding, this place really is—"

"A pile of ash? I know," chuckled Christopher.

She detected some pride in his voice.

"So, it just—hasn't been touched?"

"Mmm, more or less," he said. "There's nothing we can do with it. It's weird now, having half of a home to look up at all day, but I don't mind."

"And, nobody comes up here?"

"Well, after the Evans family escaped, we eventually had people wanting to know what they had been keeping in their house all this time. They didn't find much. Whatever they did have was either in protected accounts or up in flames."

"Right."

The entire story of what happened after they passed out had been explained to Beverly and Simon through long phone calls with Christopher once Milhaven was far, far away. He told them that, after they were both dragged away from the fire by Daniel's shaking hands and a couple of strangers, the townspeople became enraged. The Evans family escaped, though nobody knew how exactly. They ran away, without addressing the townspeople, without taking their valuables. They just ran.

Beverly had asked Christopher why the Evans family had done nothing in retaliation. She couldn't figure it out. They had both money and resources on their side, and they still just gave up.

Christopher and Simon both knew why. The Evans family survived off of the power they were given by the townspeople through their silence. The people wouldn't accept that arrangement anymore. The Evanses had no more power; there was nothing left for them in Milhaven.

"I can't believe you did all this," Beverly said.

"I was just the one who spoke on the radio," Christopher said.

"And now, everyone's free because of it."

Christopher didn't react. It was true, his words over his parent's radio station had saved so many people. But not Caroline. The evils that plagued the town like a tumor took Caroline from him. It was little consolation that the Evans family had left. Even though they abandoned the town, and a sense of peace had been restored, Caroline would never be around to see it.

Christopher's grieving process would be a long one. It would involve many lonely nights and many visits from Simon to Milhaven, as well as trips to the big city to see Beverly and Simon. Simon thought it would have made Caroline happy if she knew what Christopher had done and that Christopher was getting out and seeing the world because of it.

Sometimes, in the middle of the night, when he would normally be awake texting Caroline, Christopher would sneak into the recording studio and speak to all the insomniacs, people having a midnight snack, and night owls in Milhaven through the radio. He spoke freely into the night, and it was the closest he knew he'd ever get to talking to her again.

Beverly couldn't bring herself, standing on a mound of rubble, to ask him if he was okay. Even if he said, 'yes,' it probably would have been a lie. She just kicked around debris while making idle small-talk. She had barely known Caroline, and Beverly didn't feel it was her right to speak about her death when she hadn't known Caroline well in life. That's why she was on the hill in the first place. While Simon went to have lunch with Caroline's parents, Christopher asked Beverly if she wanted to go on a walk and see what was left of the Evans's house. It was a small kindness.

Christopher, at the beginning of the walk, asked Beverly if she was sure she felt comfortable seeing it. He thought she was afraid; she wasn't afraid at all, to see the house or to go back to the town for the first time in months, but there was a reason it had taken her over a year. Everyone was telling her it was safe, but the strength of her memories—the bad memories— kept her from returning. Mara and Simon understood her apprehension. Daniel understood her apprehension and encouraged her to take her time. She didn't need Daniel to take care of her anymore but was glad to become his friend. Beverly loved watching her uncle thrive outside of Milhaven, far away from the Evans family's grasp, which he once believed was his only option. She knew that he was stronger than he thought. They made a promise to stay in one other's lives.

After Beverly left town for good, she reunited with Mara. She spent months recuperating emotionally, spending all her time with her foster mom, who meant more to her than she could say. She lived with Mara for months before her acceptance into art school. When it was time for her to move away, Mara chose to move to a smaller town for the final chapters of her life, to a nursing home, her last adventure. She passed away after Beverly's first school term.

It was hard for Mara to hear about what happened in Milhaven, to know that it was because of her choices, fears, and insecurities that Beverly experienced so much harm. She'd had no idea she was sending Beverly to such a dangerous place.

We can only ever do what we believe is right in the moment, and Mara had believed that Milhaven was a challenge Beverly could handle. She'd lived long enough to learn that she was right.

Though she emerged from it relatively unscathed, the town of Milhaven had changed Beverly forever. She and Simon spent a lot of time together after they both left town in a makeshift ambulance, talking about the traumas they experienced in the town of Milhaven, as if they were just old school friends catching up over the good old days. They had so much in common already, and their experiences in Milhaven were just one more thing to talk about.

Moving away from Milhaven changed everything between Simon and Beverly. While still in town, just speaking to her had been difficult for Simon. He had known he was going to fall for her, but that she was going to be gone again soon enough. He didn't want a relationship back then. He did want to know her, to learn about her, and to spend time with her to see what might happen next—to slowly align like a sun and moon at an eclipse—but he couldn't have asked her for that. That would have meant she had attached to the town, and Simon believed Beverly was never meant to live in Milhaven—that she deserved more. Loving her would have been the most selfish thing he ever did. He had made himself a promise to never offer himself to someone who, in the end, deserved more than he could give.

That was a promise he tried to keep. But, upon leaving Milhaven and making a new life with her in the city, his feelings for Beverly became transparent, like fabric being stretched thin. Beverly had fallen just as hard as he did. Despite Simon's promise to keep himself away, Beverly's feelings blossomed anyway, because love is a thing that happens whether or not you feel you deserve it.

Christopher walked slowly through the rubble, rambling on to Beverly about the recent goings-on of Milhaven.

"And, there's a new mayor, too. The old one had the sense to leave when the Evans family did. Thank God for that. Then the old guidance counsellor, he ran, and he got elected," Christopher said.

"That's great."

"Hey, um … before we meet with Simon and get to my house, is it okay if we drop by the post office? There's something there I need to show you."

"Uh, yeah. Yeah, sure, of course."

"Great." Christopher smiled.

Beverly looked down at the rest of Milhaven from the top of the hill. It looked just as dull and dormant as she thought it did when she first moved to the town. How wrong she had been. She now knew that the town of Milhaven was as complex and alive as the human heart. She could do nothing but marvel at it for still beating.

She turned and looked down. On the path between the woods, at the bottom of the hill, was Simon, walking up with a wave. She wasn't running away this time. Looking down at Simon, on that patch of unburned grass, it was perhaps the first time she felt as though she had a future worth running toward.

Author photograph by Ritche Perez.

Jessica Casey is a young author who discovered her passion for writing at an early age. She's an avid baker, public speaker and aerialist with a habit of thinking up new worlds to write in her free time. Though she'll be heading off to university soon after *The Runaway's Promise* is published, she'll always call Paradise, Newfoundland her home.

Lightning Source UK Ltd.
Milton Keynes UK
UKHW020856290820
369029UK00010B/419